KT-428-379
www.susan-hill.com
80003360176

ALSO BY SUSAN HILL

Fiction

Gentleman and Ladies
A Change for the Better
I'm the King of the Castle
The Albatross and Other Stories
Strange Meeting
The Bird of Night
A Bit of Singing and Dancing
In the Springtime of the Year
The Woman in Black
Mrs De Winter
The Mist in the Mirror
Air and Angels
The Service of Clouds
The Boy Who Taught the Beekeeper to Read
The Man in the Picture
The Beacon
The Small Hand
A Kind Man
Dolly

The Simon Serrailler Cases

The Various Haunts of Men
The Pure in Heart
The Risk of Darkness
The Vows of Silence
The Shadows in the Street
The Betrayal of Trust
A Question of Identity
The Soul of Discretion

Non-Fiction

The Magic Apple Tree
Family
Howards End is on the Landing

For Children

The Battle for Gullywith
The Glass Angels
Can it be True?

SUSAN HILL

Black Sheep

VINTAGE BOOKS
London

Published by Vintage 2014

2 4 6 8 10 9 7 5 3 1

First published in Great Britain in 2013 by Chatto & Windus

Vintage
Random House, 20 Vauxhall Bridge Road,
London SW1V 2SA

www.vintage-books.co.uk

Addresses for companies within The Random House Group Limited can be found at: www.randomhouse.co.uk/offices.htm

The Random House Group Limited Reg. No. 954009

A CIP catalogue record for this book is available from the British Library

ISBN 9780099539568

The Random House Group Limited supports the Forest Stewardship Council® (FSC®), the leading international forest-certification organisation. Our books carrying the FSC label are printed on FSC®-certified paper. FSC is the only forest-certification scheme supported by the leading environmental organisations, including Greenpeace. Our paper procurement policy can be found at: www.randomhouse.co.uk/environment

Printed and bound by CPI Group (UK) Ltd, Croydon, CR0 4YY

For Penelope Hoare
Best of Editors for half a lifetime.

PART ONE

I

ON MONDAYS, the village, which was called Mount of Zeal, smelled of washing as well as of coal dust. By the time the children were walking to school, kitchens and sculleries were full of steam, and suds drifted out of the open doors of Lower Terrace and rose to join those from Middle Terrace, and then Upper Terrace, known as Paradise.

Mount of Zeal was built in a bowl like an amphitheatre, with the pit winding gear where a stage would be. The pit lay deep below it all.

Once, when Ted Howker was four, he had asked why, if Upper Terrace was called Paradise, the pit was not called Hell. Evie had boxed his ears and told him she would wash his mouth out with soapsuds if he ever said such a thing again and her face had such a power of meaning on it that he had not, but the power did not extend to his thoughts and imaginings, and sometimes at night his dreams were lurid with flames.

'It comes from your grandfather,' Evie said, 'it comes from what you have heard him read out loud all these years.' But Ted knew that her power did not extend in that direction either.

School was on the far edge of Lower, next to the chapel. It took nine minutes to walk there, and on his first two mornings Evie had taken him, his hand clamped in hers. On the third morning, Rose had walked him, leaving his hand free. She had finished senior school the previous summer and had no position, nor the prospect of one.

On the fourth morning, and on every one after that for the rest of his school life, Ted had been sent off alone, as had happened to his brothers years before him. In no time he had learned where others emerged from their own houses and he joined up with them on this or that corner, and with more as they came from Paradise and Middle Terrace, down the steep hill, while the older ones went the reverse way, joining at corners and then climbing the hill to the larger school.

Now, Ted was eight, rising nine, and confident, no longer the youngest child to walk with his snap tin held under his arm.

It was mid-September, warm, and the sky above Mount of Zeal was an Italian painter's blue, as revealed in the postcards pinned on the walls of the school corridor by Miss Irons, who loved Art. But the village saw little of the Italian painters' gilded light, which could rarely pierce through the pall of soot.

It was Monday and the suds hung on the still air, never rising higher than Middle Terrace, but eventually just evaporating there.

'You can help,' Evie Howker said. Then raised her voice. 'I know what you're doing, Rose.'

She had heard the bump of the trunk lid on the floor above, however quietly Rose had tried to open it.

She would have shouted again and in a voice not to be denied, but something inside her softened for a moment and she let her daughter be. She stood to rest her arms on the washtub. It would all come to Rose soon enough as it was, the piles of bedding and blackened shirts and vests, the baby muslins and the metal tub of grey water.

Evie edged round the tub to lean instead on the door frame, looking out, the suds wreathing round her head.

Mount of Zeal rose in steps to Paradise and then ended, after a short incline, apparently having reached the sky itself, though only because the hill was too steep to reveal the open land beyond. After that, tracks led across country, one to Mount of Zeal farm, a mile and a half away, the others to the sheep moors, spreading and clambering across stony outcrops.

Her mother could not have heard the trunk opening. Perhaps she did not know about her interest in the trunk at all, was Rosie's thought whenever she went to it. The first layer was of two folded winter blankets, the next of saved baby clothes, all for a girl. There had been four boys and by the time the clothes had got down to Ted, the afterthought, they were all wear and patches, but Rose was the only daughter. Her infant and small-girl clothes formed a beautifully washed and pressed and folded layer, with sheets of brown paper separating them from the bedding.

Now, she moved them aside carefully. *Did* her mother know? Rose had never seen her look in the trunk other than to take out the winter blankets when the weather hardened. At the very bottom were two hand-embroidered pillowcases and a small white tablecloth with drawn threadwork, all given to Rose by her Great-Aunt Etta, a few days before she had died.

'You put them safe away.' Her paper-dry hand had pressed down on Rose's soft young one.

'Never used, never once. I kept them for my own bottom drawer and bottom drawer was where they stayed, there being no marriage.'

'Why not?' Rose had not yet grown embarrassed to ask such things openly. In her mind, her great-aunt's would-be husband must have been killed in the war or died of a wasting disease or a tropical fever.

'No man ever asked me.'

Which had silenced her. She had stared at the old face and chin warts and bristle, into the flat, discoloured eyes, half hidden deep below the lids, and the flaking baldness through the veil of hair, and although of course she had known in her head that Etta had once been young and without these defects, the 94-year-old and youth had still been unimaginable partners.

'I might have had more. I don't remember. I know I had towels. I must have given those away. I had a satin nightdress case and I did give that away, once it was clear my chance had gone. I don't know why I kept these. I don't remember. You should have them, Rose, for your bottom drawer. You can never begin too soon, there's so much to gather, or how is a married home to be started? Your chances are all waiting ahead of you.'

When she had got home to Lower Terrace with the parcel, her mother had been out helping a neighbour newly home from hospital, so Rose had been able to take the things upstairs and hide them in the trunk that also served as a clothes horse and a seat in the front bedroom. It was not a secretive nature but only embarrassment that had made her want the things kept from Evie, at least for the time being. A 'bottom drawer' had a meaning beyond itself, to do with things of which Rose was only just becoming fully aware and with which she was not yet at ease.

The house was quiet, save for the bump and churn of the washtub. Her mother had called her but she had pretended not to hear. She had just a minute or two to herself and such minutes were rare enough. The men were always on different shifts and if two were nights then the bedrooms were crammed full of sleepers. Ted got home from school at half past four and people came in and out. Minutes to yourself in a quiet house were precious and to be savoured for this reason.

Rose lifted up the winter blankets, reached under the baby clothes, and felt about for her pillowcases and the tablecloth. She would not risk bringing them out to the light, just liked to feel the raised embroidery under her fingers and the smooth edges of the threadwork round the silky cotton. She wished she had some way of adding to them, or even of having a real drawer kept specially for those things. She pictured how the cloth would be on the tea table, laid with best china for a visitor, pillowcases puffed up and gracing a wide bed.

She was sixteen. Perhaps she would be married in two years and that was not long in which to gather her linen together.

'Who is it to be, Rose?' her grandmother always asked. 'Jenny Keele has a couple of fine lads.'

But Rose would not be drawn, though she always shook her head at any mention of the Keeles, Norman and Mart, hulks of boys, who had been two years ahead of her in school and were now pushing the heaviest carts and swinging the pickaxes to start new coal seams. She was frightened of the very idea that she might marry a Keele. They came to the monthly dances looking scrubbed and smart like the rest and then Rose had sometimes given them a slightly longer scrutiny. But they were like bears, broad and huge-handed. Even in best white shirts and shoes, not boots, they alarmed her and she was happy for any of the others, Sal, Annie or Lily Harris, to be led out to dance by them and have their feet trodden on by great clumping heavy ones.

'Rose!'

She smoothed out the blankets, closed the trunk without bumping the lid, and went down to the scullery.

Evie handed the mangling over to her. John Howker, Jimmy and Clive would be back at half two from their shift and wanting dinner. Arthur, the eldest, was on nights, which he had preferred from the start, out at six thirty, home at four. He liked the walk home from the pithead best, he always said, through dark and silent streets. It was hot in the mine, but at four in the morning, the village was always cool, even in July and August, and bitter cold in winter. That was the only thing Rose knew for sure about Arthur, the silent brother, that he liked the cold and the night around him. He was the only one who came home alone into the sleeping house, sat at the table by himself, eating the dinner left for him. Evie would have stayed up, altered her pattern of sleeping so that she could help him take off his pit clothes and his boots, serve his dinner, hand him his night things, set his boots out to clean. Other mothers did, and wives and sisters and daughters. Evie felt guilty at being in bed when Arthur got back, even though it was not her fault, but what he insisted on. As a small child, he had liked to take his dinner into the scullery to eat alone, if he could get away with it, and when he had walked to school carrying his bait tin, he had never joined up at the corners with any of the others, just walked on by himself.

She had given up worrying about him now.

'Look at it like this,' John had said once, 'he's never going to leave here to wed, he's never going to strike up a conversation with any girl, he'll be bringing his wage home till the time comes when he hangs up his boots.'

'And then what? Two great pairs of legs stuck out of the chairs for me to trip over half the day.'

But the idea that she would never be left on her own had been soothing.

She put cold potatoes on to fry up and the cold joint out to slice. Monday dinner. Rose mangled. The kitchen smelled of hot wet sheets and the sun came out over the top of Paradise and slanted down onto the brick wall.

Rose had a fine head of hair, she thought, watching her daughter straighten up to haul a sheet from the tub, thick hair and wavy and gleaming like conkers.

Evie knew full well about the pillowcases and tablecloth, because Aunt Etta had told her, and besides, Rose had not been as quiet as she'd supposed, the bottom of the trunk always scraped on the floor however silently she tried to open and close the lid. She wondered why Rose wanted to keep it secret. She was only a few years off being a respectable age to marry and every other girl started a bottom drawer. When the time came, she herself had some things stored away to give to her, as her own mother had done for her. But Rose was not like the rest of them, any more than Arthur was, and it sometimes troubled Evie that she had given rise to two what you might call 'misfits' – though never for long, because her days were too full.

She carved the meat into slices, and the end bit into three small chunks. The apple pie was untouched, as she always baked two identical, one for hot at Sunday lunch, the other for cold supper Monday, and a slice for Ted's bait. Ted. She had wondered if he would be another misfit but he seemed to be growing up ordinarily, joining up with friends on the corner, playing out with them, thumping and getting thumped, asking John about the pit. It hovered on the farthest edges of Evie's mind sometimes, that Ted ought to have something else to look forward to than the pit, something better, more . . . what? Adventurous, she had once answered herself, and almost laughed aloud. What would anyone do with an adventure? Ted was up to where he ought to be at school, though no further. He was growing, though he was still alarmingly thin, he chattered, he scabbed his knees and banged his head, like the rest of them. Ted would not be a misfit and marriage to the right boy would set Rose back in the fold, too. It was only Arthur.

'Rose, haven't you got the last of those whites out of the tub yet? It's gone twelve. Come here, I'll take them, you can do the privy scrub. And don't look at me like that, girl.' For Evie felt a rush of impatience with her daughter, standing with her hands still on the tub, looking at nothing out of the door. What was life about?

At five, the washing for Alice was ready to be carted up to Paradise, on the pram. Evie had done her mother-in-law's washing as well as her own for the last three weeks, because Alice was weak in some way, couldn't lift her arms properly and got white with tiredness. 'I'm beyond tired,' she had said several times. Evie understood. Tiredness was usual, especially at the end of every working week, your entire body was cried out with tiredness. But a night's deep sleep without having to set the alarm on Sunday morning generally sorted it out. Alice looked as if the tiredness had settled in the marrow of her bones.

'What's wrong with Alice?' Evie had asked her father-in-law. 'Has she said anything? Have you asked her? Have you even noticed?'

But Reuben Howker noticed nothing. 'She says she's ailing somehow.'

'Yes, but what-how?'

He shook his head, turning his eyes back to the Book. 'She's not very swift about the place.'

Evie could have shaken him until his brains rattled, could have picked him up and kicked him out of the door and down the hill from Paradise to Lower and on down to the pit, which he had left one day nine years before and never returned to, saying he had seen the Devil below and been tempted, saying he could never go back for fear of losing his soul. Evie had wanted to shake him that day and every day after. His description of the Devil had been vivid and horrifying, others had murmured their sympathy, some had crossed the street to avoid being in any form of contact with him, and many had thought he should have been sent away. Only Evie, and perhaps John, though his conscience half told him he should side with his father, refused to believe any of it. Reuben had always hated the pit and been off sick whenever he could manage it, sustained this or that generally invisible injury, had left the work to Alice and sat in the corner with his Bible all day and half the night. Only Evie had had the nerve to call him idle to his face.

If it had not been for Alice, she would never have set foot in their house again, and instructed her family to do likewise. But she loved Alice, who was tested beyond human endurance and put up with it all meekly, she would help Alice while she had strength in her body, and her family followed suit.

'Rose!' But as Ted had come in from school, Rose had slipped out of the door and vanished like a soap bubble when it touched the door frame. So Ted would come with her, pushing the old pram by holding one side of the handle while Evie held the other. 'You're as good as that lump of a sister any day,' Evie said, though in truth it was harder on her to have just him lending his weight, because there was so little of it. Ted was thin enough to go through a crack in the door, and pale-skinned, fair-haired, like a wraith. But he pushed without complaint or suggesting a pause and together they manoeuvred the pram full of clean washing up the steep path to number 8 Paradise.

Rose had weighed it up and decided the risk was worthwhile. She resented being the only girl and so the only skivvy, with her mother, to five males, while knowing perfectly well that it was usual.

Mary Roberts was on the corner of Middle, near the last house before the track that led to the school. They sneaked through the side gate of the chapel and came out in the stretch of open grass where the youngest kids had playtime in fine weather. Nobody else was about.

'I got one,' Mary said, grinning to show her black front tooth, and dived into her pocket for the cigarette, which was slightly flattened and ragged where tobacco was pulling out of the end. The matches were hidden in the bole of the single tree that stood beside the gate.

It was Mary who had started it, bringing a cigarette from her father's pocket one day the previous summer. It had taken Rose a long time to get used to the taste and the smell, and even now, she felt sick for the first few puffs, though she would never have admitted it. None of the men in her own house smoked, apart from her father, who had a single pipe every Saturday night. Mary's mother and elder sister smoked, it was easy to get hold of them furtively.

They leaned against the tree, taking turns at the cigarette, holding it out on an extended arm between first fingers, or cupped backwards in their palms, getting the feel.

They said nothing. No one was about. The Monday suds had dissolved away now. The pit smoke clouded the air and the smoke from their cigarette, wispy and pale, couldn't hold out against it.

'I saw Harry,' Rose said, looking right away from Mary. 'He was with Roy.'

Mary said nothing. It was her turn for the cigarette.

'They'll be there together then. I expect.'

'I expect.'

Harry Murdon and Roy James, the same age as Arthur, but there the likeness began and ended. Arthur would never have gone to the Institute Saturday night, nor learned how to eye a girl without appearing to, nor had a close friend.

Rose threw the cigarette down, disliking the strong smell of the butt end on her fingers, and ground it with her heel.

'You'll be for it,' Mary said.

'So will you.'

They burst out laughing.

2

'*THY WORD is a lamp unto my feet and a light unto my path.*'

Reuben sat in the corner of the room, the Bible open on his knee. Ted sat on the window ledge, looking down the slopes to the top of the pit winding gear, just visible from here. If he went and stood on the front step of 8 Paradise, he could see it clearly.

'*For he is our God and we are the people of his pasture and the sheep of his land.*'

His grandfather's voice rumbled on and the murmurings of his mother and grandmother in the room above formed a lighter descant to it.

'Do you have anything you can say, our Ted?'

Ted struggled. They had a Bible reading every morning at the start of school, and a Religious Instruction class once a week, but he never remembered much, though he liked the sound of the words, as he liked to hear his grandfather read the Bible aloud, since it was the earliest sound he could remember, and so a familiar comfort to him.

'*Before the mountains were settled before the hills was I brought forth*,' Ted said, closing his eyes to help him remember right.

His grandfather grunted.

Ted looked at him, then out of the window again.

'You give me chapter and verse, boy, chapter and verse.'

But Ted could not.

The voices of the two women went on like a bubbling stream above.

When he was a baby, in the pram that they had just pushed up the slopes full of clean washing, Ted had been put with his grandfather and left to listen to the words of the Bible, which Reuben read day and night, sometimes in silence, often aloud. The deep voice and the words had been the background to Ted's waking and sleeping, and as he grew older, to his pottering about the room, in and out of the door, back again, clambering over the steep step. The voice had always been there, like the air and the light.

'*I made me pools of water, to water therewith the wood that bringeth forth trees.*'

He did not know the meaning of the words but they slipped over him, wrapping him in an assurance of safety even when they were in the Old Testament's most thundering and vengeful strain.

At eight now, he understood a little more and sometimes longed for a phrase or two of gentleness. He wanted to ask questions too, but knew better, for Reuben would never answer except with another river of words.

Ted leaned his head against the pane and watched for the file of men to come trailing up the slope at the end of their shift.

In the bedroom above, Evie sat on the straight-backed chair beside the bed.

'Well, if you won't show me at least describe to me what it's like.'

Alice's back was turned away from her. She fidgeted constantly with the button on her blouse.

'Don't tell him,' she said for the hundredth time. 'Don't say a word.'

'I've promised, haven't I? Am I a liar?'

Silence.

'He knows there's something wrong, Alice.'

'What has he said?'

Evie hesitated, then repeated the one thing. 'That you're not very swift about the place. Which is plain for all to see.'

'I seem to have no stuffing left in me.'

'I can tell.'

Alice had lost more weight. Not that she had ever been stout. The flesh seemed to have peeled off her bones and the skin hung loose.

'If you'd show me.'

'I've shown no one. I get dressed and undressed in the dark.'

Evie tutted, and then decided. She got up and went to stand in front of the other woman, took Alice's hands in hers and held them firmly away, then started to undo the buttons of her blouse, from the top. Alice took a breath, then let it go. Let Evie carry on.

She opened the blouse carefully. Alice sighed.

The swelling was the size of an apricot, pushing against the skin. Evie pulled her hand away sharply.

'Oh, Alice.'

Alice's expression was blank but when Evie looked into her eyes she saw fear there.

'You have to see the doctor. You have to go at once. Go tomorrow.'

Alice shook her head and started to put her clothing straight again.

'I know what it is, Evie, I know there's nothing he can do or say. And so do you if you'll be truthful.'

Evie did know.

She put her hand on the other woman's arm and rested it there, and so they stood, both silent, as if they were staring into the depths of the same river but from opposite banks.

3

During the weeks going into that winter, Mary took up with Charlie Minns, whose father was one of the pit inspectors and lived in a house set apart from the terraces, and after that, although Rose saw her here and there, things were never the same between them and there were no more sneaked half-hours with giggling and cigarettes. But one afternoon when it was wet and the sky seemed to have been lowered, to hang heavy over the village, Rose was sent to the shop to buy extra flour and there was Mary, in a new skirt and woollen jacket, and with her hair curled up. Rose took a step back as she saw her, uncertain and tongue-tied.

Mary looked her up and down and shifted her neck a little inside the collar of the new jacket. She was buying soap.

'Would you wrap it please?'

Mrs Leather gave her a hard look, which pleased Rose.

'Your mam never asks. I don't have wrapping paper to burn.'

Mary put her hand up and pulled the lapel of the jacket straighter.

She doesn't want to be seen carrying soap, Mrs Leather's look said to Rose.

'Oh, never mind.' Mary put the money down and took up the soap bar, holding it slightly away from her.

'Hello, Mary,' Rose said, quite at ease now.

Mary stopped. 'Oh, Rose . . . I didn't catch sight of you there. How are you getting on?'

'Very well, thank you.'

'I'm so busy I don't have much time to see anyone these days. Why don't you come to the Institute on Saturday night? We don't always go there now, me and Charlie, we like to venture a bit further afield, you know how it is, but we'll go Saturday, show you who's who. Will you?'

I know very well who's who, Rose wanted to say, I went to school with them all, didn't I? And so did you.

'I must fly, get this bloomin' soap home before Charlie comes round.'

'Goodbye then.'

As she was closing the shop door, hand on the latch, Mary said again, 'You will come, Rose?'

There was something in her voice.

'I'll try,' Rose said and turned to Mrs Leather to ask for the flour.

She said nothing more, but when she got out of the shop, saw Mary hovering a few yards ahead. She wanted to swish past her, head in the air, but she knew she would never bring off such a gesture, so all she did was walk as if she was not going to stop.

'Wait, Rosie.'

Rose waited, out of surprise at being called Rosie, the name she had left behind at primary school. But she waited for Mary to do any of the talking.

'Will you come?'

'I don't think so.'

'You'd have a good time. It's fun. We'd look after you.'

'I don't need you to look after me.'

'You know what I mean. I'm sorry I haven't seen you lately.'

'No you're not. You know where I live, I haven't moved.'

They neared the house before either spoke again.

'You've changed,' Mary said then.

'No, you have. A pit inspector's son is higher up in the world. You have to wear grander clothes.'

'Rosie . . .'

'I'm not Rosie.'

'I thought it might be all right, I thought you were a real friend. Real friends don't take on just because of who I'm going out with. How can I help what job his dad does?'

'You can't. But what job does Charlie do? I think he's training up to be the same, isn't he? I don't think he's in the black hole at the bottom of the pit shaft like ours.'

Rose felt ashamed of herself for saying it, but now it was said, she did not know how to take it back, though she saw the look on Mary's face, of hurt and unhappiness.

'Bye then, Mary.' It was the best she could do. She lifted her hand in a half-wave, as she went in the door. But she didn't look round.

The house was thick with the smell of coal dust and the heat of the men's bodies, the kitchen smaller by half now three of them were back and digging in round the table, with Ted as usual kneeling on the window ledge looking out and Evie banging pans.

'You been milling that flour or what?'

'Sorry. I met Mary and she kept me talking.'

'No one keeps you talking if you don't want to be kept and don't waste your breath on those that act high and mighty.'

'No, she doesn't. It's not her fault what job he does. Why shouldn't he? Someone's got to be a pit inspector.'

'I hope your dad didn't hear that.'

'I heard it.' John rumbled from the table. But he had his mouth full of meat-and-potato pie and was not really roused.

Jimmy would go to bed straight after tea. Arthur was on late shift with his father. Evie and Rose cleaned the boots, put out two fresh shirts, made up the bait tins. The door stood open to let in some air. But summer was worst, Rose thought, banging the brush on the step before starting on the next boot, August when the sun might hammer down on Mount of Zeal for two or three weeks at a time and the houses smelled of sweat and breath and feet and smuts, and every door and window from Lower to Paradise stood open day and night.

'I dare say Mary will be wed to him,' Evie said now, giving her a sharp look. Rose shrugged. 'And no reason why not. One way of bettering yourself.'

'And leaving your old friends behind.'

'Well, what would you do?'

'I wouldn't marry Charlie. He squints.'

'Doesn't make him a bad lad.'

'It makes him ugly.' Rose set the last boot down on the floor.

'So who are you picking to get out the pillowcases for?'

Rose was angry, not only for what Evie had said, but for not being able to stop herself flushing up scarlet. She turned away and would have got out of the room, but for Clive sticking his leg in front of her and almost having her on the floor. She heard them all roaring with laughter, saw their faces, mouths open and full of tea and pie, and as well as being red in the face, she was in tears as well, hating to be laughed at.

Only Ted, still looking out of the window, was apart from the scene.

'Leave the girl,' John Howker said, scraping his plate, 'let her alone.' But he was good-humoured, and never serious about chastising them where Rose was involved. Rose was fair game.

Husband and wife had precious little time to talk privately. Evie was getting this or that man off to his shift or sorting them out the minute they got back. No one went and came at the same regular time. And so it was not until four days later that she had a chance to talk to him about his mother.

'How do you mean, "it looks bad"?'

'Will you hear? She showed it to me. She has a lump on her – her breast, like a gull's egg.'

'How did she start up a boil there?'

'Not a boil.'

'Oh, all right then.' He turned over.

'Your mother has a cancer.'

'Now how do you know that?'

'I saw it, John.'

He was silent. The whole room was full of the silence and the weight of what she had said lay upon it.

'I don't know what she's to do. I'm taking the washing. Rose'll help me. Reuben's fit for nothing. She hasn't told him a word.'

After a few moments she reached out and touched John's arm and kept her hand there. She felt him, silent, thinking it over, letting what it meant sink down, and then she felt his body fall heavy into sleep.

4

THAT AUTUMN and early winter Alice Howker lay dying and whenever he did not have to be at school Ted was with her. He fetched anything she might want, which was precious little, and otherwise sat quietly on the floor beside the big bed, or stood at the window looking down over the whole of Mount of Zeal, and lights in the terraces from every house, in Paradise, Middle and Lower. It was dark now when the men came up from the five o'clock. Ted saw lights from the pithead and the file of them trudging away from it and home.

'I shan't see you into double figures,' his grandmother said, out of nowhere, one late afternoon. The oil lamp was on, tallow light falling onto her face, finding out the hollows and making the bones gleam under the yellow skin.

Ted turned from the window. He knew what she meant but could think of nothing to say.

'You're the best of boys.' The words were barely carried to him on her thin breath. She was tired from morning to night now, though she barely slept. 'You know what I'm saying?'

Ted nodded.

'You're . . .' She sighed and closed her eyes. He watched her eyelids flutter occasionally as she dozed and her hand twitch as it rested on the sheet. He went back to the window. The pit winding gear showed like gallows against the last red of the sky.

He heard the back door close, his mother's voice, his grandfather's, the two weaving in and out, bass and descant. Footsteps on the stairs.

'I'll see to Alice.'

Ted went down.

Reuben was sitting in his chair by the stove, as usual. He rarely moved from it now.

'I could prod his great idle backside with a pitchfork,' Evie had said.

'*There was a man in the land of Uz whose name was Job, and that man was perfect and upright and one that feared God and eschewed evil.*'

Ted listened to the words rolling like thunder round the room. He knew these well though they were not his favourites.

He said, '*And the Angel of the Lord appeared unto him, in a flame of fire out of the midst of a bush, and he looked, and behold, the bush burned with fire, and the bush was not consumed.*'

Reuben looked up. 'Go on.'

Ted shook his head.

'Go on . . .'

Ted gathered the words together, knitting them up into the verses gradually. Reuben waited, his finger marking the page in the black Bible.

'*And Moses said, I will now turn aside, and see this great sight, why the bush is not burnt. And when the Lord saw that he turned aside to see, God called unto him out of the midst of the bush, and said, Moses, Moses. And he said, Here am I.*'

In the bedroom, Evie was lifting the dressing off the sore on Alice's breast, which was now like an egg whose shell had broken open. She tried not to turn away from the sight and the smell, knowing how hurtful such a move was, knowing Alice's eyes never left her face but searched for the smallest clue as to how it looked, how much worse it seemed, what Evie was thinking but would never say.

When the dressing was done, and the foul one put into a bag to be carried away, and Alice was as comfortable as she would ever be now, against the freshly plumped pillows, Evie took her hand.

'I can't go on doing this. It isn't my place, it isn't my job. I'm not the right person.'

Fear widened Alice's eyes and she clutched at Evie.

'I must send for the doctor, Alice. He'll see what needs to be done.'

'I'm not going away.'

'They'd know how to make you comfortable. They know what's needed. I don't.'

'I'm not going into the infirmary. I'd never come out.'

'The doctor can get the nurse to come to you. They're very good.'

Alice turned her head away.

Reuben would not consider the doctor coming if Alice didn't agree. He hated strangers in the house, but most of all, he would not accept that his wife was ill in any serious way. 'She'll be about any day now. She's never been ill in all our years.'

'That isn't true and how do you have the face to say it?' Alice had been ill with every one of her children, ill before, ill during, at death's door twice after. She had been told by the doctor and the midwife, after her second, that she was risking her life, but she had gone on to five, two of which babies had died. She had been ill with pleurisy, migraine headaches, phlebitis, inflammation of the kidneys. She had struggled with everyday life for so long it had become a matter of habit for the family to help her out, though in the end it had all been left to Evie, to whom it had always been plain that Reuben had vied with his wife for attention and to be put off from work sick. It had not taken him long, and then he had assumed his seat in the front room with the black Bible, for good.

'If he comes up here he'll be sent away.'

'Have you looked at her breast, Reuben?'

'I have not.'

'Then you do. You look. It's an open suppurating sore and it'll be the death of her. It's eating her flesh away, and it won't be long before it eats to the bone, if she doesn't die first.'

Ted looked across at his mother, shocked at what he had heard, imagining something eating his grandmother 'to the bone'. He did not understand the nature of it, wondered if it was a worm that burrowed or an insect with mandibles that had somehow gained entrance to her body. On the way down the hill, he asked.

'You wouldn't want to know.'

'I do want to know. Ma?'

'Cancer, the crab,' Evie said between tight lips.

* * *

In the coal- and chalk-dust-smelling classroom the following day, he asked again.

'That's a funny question Ted Howker.' The teacher was good at drawing and in a moment, there was a crab, pincers and shell, on the blackboard.

'Who has ever seen one of these? Which lucky one of you has been to the seaside?'

A hand went up. 'But I never saw that.'

'Do you know any other sea creatures with shells? Which one of you has heard of a lobster?'

Ted sat silent in the third row back, not able to ask again, still left empty of answers as to why his grandmother's illness had set off a board full of odd chalk drawings. He turned it over in his mind all day, all the way home, half the night, over and over, as the sea turns a pebble, but got no nearer to knowing.

'Take this up to Paradise, and keep it in the basket, it's hot.' Evie wrapped a loaf and a teacake into a clean dishcloth. It was Friday afternoon. The terraces were sprinkled about with boys he knew, leaning against walls. There was a game of fives he could have joined but he had to ask his question and the basket was heavy.

Reuben was in his permanent place. '*Behold and see if there is any sorrow like my sorrow, which is done unto me.*'

Ted put the basket on the table and would have asked his question then, but there was a sound on the stairs.

He did not know the woman in the blue coat and hat who came in. Reuben fetched up a sigh that Ted thought could have come from the belly of the whale.

'Better send the boy out. I need to tell you things.'

'Go up and see your grandmother,' Reuben said.

Ted hesitated. The woman nodded her head to the stairs. 'But she's not very well, don't you give her any grief.'

He never forgot the sight of walking quietly into the front bedroom and seeing his grandmother in the high brass bed, flat under the sheets and with her head seeming to be smaller, shrunken like an apple left out in the bowl too long, and with the tears running down her cheeks.

He stood still and looked at her, but at first she did not see him, just went on crying silently, unmoving. The voices of the woman and Reuben came murmuring from below.

'Should I get you something?'

She turned her head on the pillow and looked at him as if she did not know where she was, or who he was, but then her eyes cleared of the confusion and she sighed. 'What are you doing, our Ted?'

'They sent me up. To see you. I could go away.'

'No, no. Come here.' Alice opened her hand and held it palm upwards towards him. Ted went nearer and put his own hand on hers.

'Is Evie there? Is John?'

He shook his head. 'I brought bread and a teacake. Should I get you a slice?'

'No. I'm not hungry. I've lost my appetite.'

'They're still warm.'

'It won't come back now.'

'What won't?'

'My appetite. Your grandfather will eat them.'

'You'll get hungry again when you're well.'

'I'm not going to be well.'

'Do you mean not ever?' He could barely believe her.

'Never.'

'I know what's wrong with you. Does it not get better?'

'What have you been told?'

But he did not dare say the word aloud in the room. Alice closed her eyes but did not let his hand go. The room had a thick, sour smell. He looked at her arm, at the scaly skin dotted here and there with pale brown patches. He looked at her face, and her thin hair. He looked for a crab shape but could not find it.

* * *

On Sunday, he went back up the hill. Alice was sleeping, but sometimes she woke and cried out with pain, or was restless, turning over and back in the bed to try and ease herself. Ted knelt on the floor in front of the window and looked out over Mount of Zeal, seeing the smoke rise from the chimneys on Lower to mingle with those above, but all going straight up cleanly into the stillness. There were few clouds.

For once, Reuben was not downstairs thundering out the lines from Job, which he was reading through aloud for the hundredth time. He had gone out, to walk heavily along the terraces to the end and the old metal bench which someone had placed there in memory of a relative, years ago. It needed painting and the metal slats were broken in a couple of places but the family had died out and no one else saw fit to mend it. Reuben sat there on Sundays while those who went to church went to church, for if he knew his scriptures inside out and by heart, he did not care to hear them read in a voice other than his own, nor be preached at by any man.

Ted could not see him from the window but he could see the thin file of dark clothed figures leaving chapel and boys he knew playing marbles in the dust bowls. When the nurse in blue arrived now she ignored him, knowing he would not come closer to the bed and stare. He sensed that his grandmother liked him to be there, though no word was ever said about it between them, he simply arrived the minute he had eaten his tea, and left when it was dark. Evie had mentioned it only once and then left him to do as he pleased. Once, his father had come up with him, huge and awkward in the room, reaching to touch his mother then drawing his hand back in case it was the wrong thing.

'I can send the others, if you'd like it.'

But Alice moved her head restlessly on the pillows. 'Ted's my company. I'm beyond the rest.'

John stayed another couple of minutes. He had no words but a murmur flowed deep beneath his silence. He bent over to kiss her and left, glancing at Ted, hesitating, but in the end saying nothing to the boy.

Evie came every day and the nurse in blue. Alice cried with pain, slept, lay without moving or turned about, hot and restless. The boy stayed with her all day that last weekend, and would not leave at night, so that it was he who went to her when she called once, and touched her when she let out a rasping few breaths, shuddered and went still.

Something seemed to happen in the room. The air lightened. He had been holding his breath tightly as if to keep it in his chest and now he let it go and it floated away from him like a feather. He had never known such silence.

5

REUBEN CAME down to live with them less than a month later. There was no room for him, and Evie had been happy to continue taking his washing up and down the slopes, and hot food under a cloth. But he had wept, for the first and only time in his life, when she had said he would be perfectly well off staying in the Paradise house on his own, and so she had had little choice. She was aware that his tears were false and selfish, and that his repeated reading aloud that a 'precious woman was worth more than rubies' was moral blackmail. But she gave in to the blackmail, Clive and Jimmy fetched down his things, the old furniture was sold for next to nothing, and Reuben moved to Lower Terrace. He came with just his clothes, his own armchair and the black Bible, but his arrival still made the walls of the already crowded house bulge outwards.

For Evie, the worst was his constant presence looming in the room. She was used to having men about, but they were men with a purpose, men who got up, went to the pit, came back, ate, drank, went to bed, slept, got up again, and at other times made themselves scarce. She felt spied upon. If she took ten minutes out to stand at the door or talk to a neighbour, Reuben saw her and she felt judged. He said nothing, but he looked on. The other men barely noticed him. They simply shifted a bit to make room and carried on as before.

For Ted, the arrival of his grandfather was the beginning of a refrain in his life which through all his years of growing up never ceased to be singing in the background. His days were shaped by the sound of his grandfather's voice speaking the Bible. He knew the cadences of the verses, the rise and fall and occasional flash and spark, the monotonous, even rumble of the lists of kings and prophets, the thunder of the voice of God. His days and the time before he slept ran in tune with the verses, and though he rarely understood most of what he heard, he absorbed the spirit and sometimes the sense, and it left its mark upon him.

6

'CLIVE, AW, come on, come with me.'

'Stop your wheedling, girl,' John Howker said amiably, but without lifting his face above the top of the paper or taking his Saturday-night pipe from his mouth.

'I said, now get off.'

'Clive . . .'

'Ask Arthur.'

'I want you.'

Arthur shuffled his feet under the table, where he was repairing a lamp. The small parts were laid out on brown paper in careful order.

'Stop mithering your brother, Rose. Clive, you can walk her to the Legion.' Evie was turning a hem.

'What girl gets her brother to walk her?'

Rose gave up. She put on the green floral frock that had been Evie's but which Evie had altered to fit her and dressed up a little with a frill round the neck and sleeves. She damped the ends of her hair so they would curl round the comb handle. It was a cold night for summer. The window was slightly open and she shut it, to keep the smell of soot out. But the smell of soot had long ago seeped into the walls and fresh air would never shift it. You tasted it in your mouth night and day until your food was seasoned with it and would have seemed strange without.

'Not later than ten,' John Howker said as she went to the door. 'Sharp.'

'*I am the Lord thy God, who brought thee out of the land of Egypt and out of the house of bondage.*'

'Yes, Grandad, thank you.'

Arthur had almost completed the reassembly of the lamp. Ted was lying on his stomach on the floor, reading an old book he had found in a barrow parked by someone's gate, with damp, yellowed pages that stuck together and a red cover whose colour had come off onto his fingers. *Adventures with the Mounties*.

Rose slipped smooth as silk out of the door. She was nervous, walking quickly along the terrace and down the slope that led to the Institute, keeping well in to the side, away from the pairs and small groups of others who were going the same way. She did not think ahead to what it would be like, only hoped that she might meet Mary, hoped she would not look foolish and make girls laugh at her behind their hands, boys turn their backs. There was a queue to go in, people funnelling through the doors and spreading out onto the path at the bottom of the steps. And then she saw Mary with Charlie just three ahead of her, and pushed her way through, to grab her by the arm. Mary shook her off without looking round.

'Mary?'

'Oh.' Mary half glanced. 'Yes. Hello, Rose.' But then she turned away and leaned in to Charlie, whispering.

Rose felt herself flush and for a halfpenny would have got out of the queue and run for home, hot with the anger and hurt of rejection and chilled by the shame of being alone. But the queue moved forward and she with it and she had no escape. She paid her money and was inside the hall, where shoes squeaked and bumped on the wooden floor and there was a stage with lights covered in red crêpe paper and a man with an accordion, another with an instrument Rose did not recognise. The room was filling. There was chatter. All the girls clustered together near the stage, with bunches of boys just inside the doors, where the bar was. Rose crept towards the girls, not looking at anyone. Mary and Charlie and another couple had moved towards the middle of the hall and were dancing, aware of being watched. Charlie was small and rat-like, Rose decided. His shiny black hair was smarmed down across his head, showing up the spots on his neck. She shuffled further in to the circle of girls.

'Rose Howker! Didn't think you were allowed down here.'

'She'll have come with Clive. Is Clive here then?'

Heads turned to the end of the room and the boys.

'No.'

'You're not on your own, Rose, you'd never.'

'Why not? It was Mary who invited me, anyway.'

Hands flew to mouths to hold back giggles.

'That one. There they are, you seen them?' A little shriek this time.

'Charlie Minns! What's she up to then?'

'What do you mean, anyway, "it was Mary who invited you"? Don't need anyone to invite you – unless it's another sort of invitation.'

The laughter exploding like that out of the group had the whole room looking round.

'She said, would I come.'

One by one, they looked or moved away or edged past her and floated off elsewhere about the room, until Rose was alone again. She would know better next time. She felt defiant.

'Rose, will you come with me? I want to go home. Please come with me, please, you're my friend and you're not enjoying it, are you, I can tell, and I can't leave on my own.'

Mary was at her side and pulling on Rose's arm, her face white, eyelids puffy. Rose looked round but no one was watching, they were eyeing each other, one end of the room slowly merging with the other, the girls sucking on drinks with straws, looking with big eyes over the tops of tumblers, the boys hanging on to beer glasses even when they had drained them.

'Please . . .'

'But what about –'

'Don't ask, don't say it.'

Outside there was no one, as soon as they had got themselves past the boys who were standing together on the step, smoking. There was a half-moon with skeins of cloud pulled across it like frayed wool. Mary held Rose's arm tightly but stumbled on the paving in high-heeled shoes that had belonged to an aunt with smaller feet. From the open Institute windows they heard the sound of the accordion.

When they were beside their old tree, in the darkness, Mary took out a packet of cigarettes, lit two. Rose saw her face in the match flare, troubled and fearful.

'Mary . . .'

'It was what he said. He said he liked me but he would have to shape me, he would have to make sure I didn't let him down in any way at all. He said otherwise it was going to be hard to show me to his family. And he pawed me and when I said I didn't like that he said I'd get used to it quick enough, because I had such a chance with him. He said what other such chance would I have for a step up in life?'

'Oh, Mary.'

'And he's right, isn't he?'

'I don't see that you should be ashamed of your family.'

The cigarette burned strongly for a moment as Mary drew on it. Rose saw her face in the red glow, taut and anxious.

'Do you like him, Mary? I mean, really?'

Mary shrugged.

'You don't then, and you can't marry someone you don't like a lot. You have to love them.'

'What do you know about it?'

There was no need to reply.

'He puts his hands where they shouldn't be.'

Rose could not ask. She had an idea where that was.

'I don't want to go back in there tonight.'

'Or any night.'

'Oh yes, I'll go next week. You can't just stop at home, can you? Come on now.'

They went arm in arm across the dark grass and stumbled at the gap in the fence separating the field from the lane, almost pulling one another over and laughing then, as if they were still eight years old and coming home from school.

Rose went through the door smiling to herself and into panic thick as smoke filling the house. John Howker had been taken ill, falling heavily as he got up from his chair and lying with his eyes rolling back into his head, his limbs twitching then going horribly still. The boys had tried to haul him up and in the end they had managed it but he sprawled loosely, so that they had to prop him against the table leg. He made no sound other than a faint snoring in his nose and mouth, and his eyes did not focus even when they rolled back to their normal position. Reuben started to read a Psalm loudly, until Evie shouted at him, then his voice fell, though he still read on. Ted pressed himself against the wall.

That night was terrible. Ted and Rose were banished to bed, Evie sat holding John's hand but every so often she got up and went to the door to look out, as if some help would come from the sky up behind Paradise. At dawn, John was very still, his hands and face cold in spite of two blankets, and Clive was made to run the six miles to a doctor, Reuben having dug out the money from a tobacco tin slipped under his chair cushion.

In the afternoon, they struggled to move John upstairs, where he lay unaware of anything, and Ted remembered his grandmother Alice's last breaths and the silence after them, and was wary. But although the doctor diagnosed a stroke and said the next hours were critical, John grew no worse and after a while it was clear that he had begun to improve. He looked about him and spoke a few muzzled words, could raise his arms an inch or two, and even eat, so long as Evie fed him from a spoon. He slept for hours, day after day, and the sleep seemed to heal him. They sat him up, propped against two pillows. He asked for one of them to read paragraphs here and there from the local paper. He asked for, and was refused, a pipe, but when Gibby Gibbon brought round a small medicine bottle of whisky, Evie let him have a well-watered tot.

Ted came and sat in the bedroom sometimes when

he returned from school, less sure now that his father was going to die.

And he did not. By autumn he was recovered enough to start a tallying job at the pithead, though it was half-time and less money. He saw the men cram into the lifts and vanish down the shaft, counted them back, ticked them on and ticked them off, and was ill-tempered and morose, though knowing well enough that luck had been with him. Then, at the end of November, Arthur broke his arm badly, trapping himself between a pit pony and the coal face. He would be useless for a whole year, they said, if not for good.

Evie grew thinner than ever and worried to her wits' end. She chivvied Ted and called Reuben a 'great bladder of wind' and stopped him from reading from the black Bible in anything but the lowest murmur.

Most of the houses in Mount of Zeal were full to the rafters with people and the most crowded were crowded with children, but this house was crowded with adults. Ted was growing too fast, taking up more of the available space and air, John Howker and Arthur were at home most of the time and Reuben never left it. Evie struggled and for the most part lost the struggle. Rose felt crushed by the weight of men.

* * *

Her mother got up before light seeped into the sky above Paradise, and shook Rose. There were only two pairs of boots, two bait tins, two sets of work clothes to be got ready now, but cleaning and supplying food seemed to double and treble.

'I can only make a loaf go so far,' Evie said. They had to keep the back door closed and locked or the gale swept cold rain into the kitchen. 'You can black the range now, Rose, while there's a sliver of room, but get Ted up before you start.'

Ted slept alternately with Clive and Arthur. Clive would be back at the end of his shift and take over Ted's place in the bed.

'Get up.' Rose pulled the covers off in one quick move to make Ted shiver. 'Where's Arthur?'

Ted shrugged, diving for his clothes in the icy room. Rose noticed the extra length of her brother's limbs.

'Hurry up, will you?'

But Ted took the same time as ever.

Rose stood at the top of the stairs. The house was quiet except for the sharp spits of rain on the windows. She waited, not wanting to begin the blacking. Ted dived past her to the scullery and the cold tap.

'Where's Arthur?' Evie said, lifting the porridge off. 'Get the bowls, Rose girl.'

'He wasn't in the bed.'

'Well, he's not here. Ted, you scrub your neck. He's either upstairs or down.'

But he was not.

The search parties of men went out after the two days and nights during which there was neither sight nor sound of Arthur. They beat the bounds of the village, scouring every corner from Lower to Paradise, and in the end, order was given to evacuate the pit, its shafts and workings, and all the above-ground buildings. He was not found, living or dead. The police put out a description and there was frantic talk of divers and of dredging, but in the end that talk and any other died away, leaving only an echo of 'when Arthur Howker vanished'.

From the age of three Ted had kept his 'findings' – small stones, a mouse skeleton, a red leaf, a forked pin or a bent coin. His father had given him an old tobacco tin and he had stored it away under a loose floorboard, which he prised open with neat fingers. By chance, he found nothing worth keeping for many months after Arthur's disappearance, but then he came upon a smooth pale flat stone with a hole through the centre, on the path leading to Middle Terrace.

When he dug out his tobacco tin later, he found Arthur's penknife inside it, wrapped in a bit of worn shirt cloth.

He held the knife very carefully, as if weighing it, and then turned it over and over in the palm of his hand. The last time he had opened the tobacco tin, his brother had still been here, using the knife to chip away at this and probe into that, and as a tool to help him with mending a lamp or a door handle.

He had not been drowned or fallen into a pit then, he had left his knife for Ted and gone away of his own accord – though how or where who knew, or ever would?

Ted sat on the upstairs window ledge and turned a question over in his mind as he had turned the knife in his hand. Should he tell or not? If he started to use the knife someone would notice before he took his next breath. But he had longed and longed to have it, begged Arthur to lend it just for a minute. Arthur never would. But now he had given it to him, no doubt at all.

In the end, Ted slipped it into his trouser pocket and kept it there, carrying it about for a whole day, never letting it see the light, but often touching it. Its touch made him feel safe. And then he put it back in the tobacco tin and the tin under the floorboard, and banged the floorboard down hard with his shoe so that he would never be able to get at it again. In that way, he felt that he could keep his brother at home and all to himself.

PART TWO

7

CHARLIE MINNS had gone after half the girls in Mount of Zeal before he settled on Rose and by then each was relieved to have found the other. Most of Rose's friends were married now, or at least spoken for, and Charlie Minns cut a poor figure among the strong swarthy pitmen. He was still thin, and though the flare of spots on his face and neck had subsided, it had left pocks and craters, and his teeth were crooked and browner than ever. Because he was from a manager's family, they got a decent house on Middle Terrace straight away. Rose was relieved it was not among the half-dozen down beside the pithead, which were cut off from the rest of the village, socially as well as in terms of position, and because they never got the sun, the rain rolled down the hills straight into them, and the film of coal dust was twice as thick on every surface. She saw the house they had been given with relief, not wanting to be separated from her own family by much more than the marriage itself had divided them.

She took the embroidered pillowcases and table-cloth out of the trunk, and had most of the sheets from Alice's old linen cupboard, which Evie had kept for her. There was money for other things from Charlie's family, though the idea that they were as rich as anyone in the world was wrong and based on simple envy and resentment, as Rose found.

The house in Lower seemed empty to Evie after Arthur's disappearance and Rose's marriage, and Jimmy's wedding only a year later too. She sat by the fire in the evenings wondering how she had coped, listening to Reuben wheeze out the readings from the black Bible, and had only John and Clive to sort out to and from the pit. But then came the summer when Ted was fourteen and left school.

'What else would you do?' his father had asked, with good reason, when he protested that he was not going down the pit. 'There's no other work.'

'Then I'll move away and find something.'

Evie had started to cry and gone on crying half the evening and into the night, so that nobody could ignore the distress of it, nothing more was said and

Ted was hired at the coal mine, starting on the first of September.

It was the hottest summer anyone had known. Doors and windows stood open day and night without a stir of air getting into the houses. Even the smallest children stayed out playing on the terraces and on the steps until midnight and a baby died of heatstroke. Layers of coal dust lay heavy over the village, and by the middle of August, there was talk of water being rationed if people were not sparing with it. Down the mine was far hotter than up above, so that the men came from their shifts drained of all energy and walked up the slope weary as driven cattle, to bath in cold water, eat, and then sit outside beside the young ones, smoking and drinking tea, too tired for conversation. Even Reuben left his chair at the back of the room and sat on a broken-down wicker one from morning to night, whispering from the Bible to any passer-by. His voice was hoarse all the time and he had a raking cough.

The Lord trieth the righteous: but the wicked and him that loveth violence his soul hateth.

'Too many years of spouting aloud,' Evie said without sympathy. 'Poor Alice. How it must have been for her I never thought.'

Ted's friends had left school and were almost all waiting for their first day at the pit, but he felt too restless and unsettled either to hang about with them or to stay in the house. He would climb up the paths to Paradise and sit on a stone outcrop looking over the countryside in the shimmering heat, then one afternoon went further on. He had not been up to the farms since he had come with Arthur once or twice when he was a young boy, and once or twice with John, after they had been to see his grandparents. But that had only been a half-mile or so up the steep track, never to the peak and beyond.

It was towards the end of a Friday afternoon, when everyone gasped for air and the sky was sulphurous, that Ted walked up the track towards Zeal Farm and then on, following the path that wound round to the west before it straightened and climbed steeply up to the peak. When he was a boy he had thought it as high as a mountain. Now, with drops of sweat running down the sides of his face as he reached the top, he realised that, after all, it was just a hill. He looked back and saw the dry grass and the roof of Zeal Farm. Looking ahead he saw that the land dropped away and then climbed to another peak, dropped away and climbed, and that there were hills as far as he could see, disappearing into the belly of the sullen sky. Sheep were scattered about the hillsides as if someone had thrown them in the air and let them fall anyhow, but their cries did not reach far, without a breath of wind to carry them. The village and the pit were not visible but the fine veil of black like a swarm of bees in the sky showed where they lay.

Ted thought that he would like to come here, lie down and sleep on the grass. On a cloudless night there might be less of a pall from the pit obscuring the moon and stars in the sky.

Twice since the date for starting at the pit had been fixed, he had spoken up about not wanting to go, but if they had listened, John and Evie Howker had not replied, and everything raced on towards his first day, like a train without brakes.

Rather than wait for a cloudless night, he lay down on the ground now, at the side of the track. The dry grass pricked through his shirt, and when he looked up, he saw that the sky was milky in the heat. No one much came up this far from the village because they felt unsafe in the wideness, without the usual bounds of houses and hill, and because they did not know what to do here or altogether trust it.

'Now then.'

A man stood over him, rough-faced and with his boots so close Ted could see the cracks and creases in the old leather. He sat up. But the man only stood looking down at him with a mild expression. 'Hot.'

Ted nodded.

'Job for them to get a drop of juice out of this.' He nodded his head to four or five sheep clumped together.

'Are they yours?'

'They are.' He nodded again, to where the land dipped down below a cleave in the hill. 'Crow's Farm. You know it?'

'No.'

'Thought you wouldn't. All right then.' He whistled and a sheepdog sprang up as if out of the ground itself and ran low to his side.

Ted watched them go. The heat haze shimmered round and then absorbed them before they had reached the dip.

That night he lay with the window wide open, the coal dust lining his nostrils. People coughed through the darkness. He got up at five and went out before the men were changing shifts. The terraces were empty, heat still coming off the house walls. One or two lights were on.

It was cooler as he climbed up the slope. Winding sheets of mist swaddled the sheep and rested in the hollow. Ted breathed easily and the soft mist damped his skin.

The sheepdog barked its warning of him while he was a hundred yards away and he saw it scurrying to and fro inside the gate to the farmyard. Smoke coiled out of the chimney.

'You again.' It was not a question.

Ted reached him and the farmer opened the gate a few inches to let him in. The dog nosed him then lay down.

'My name's Ted Howker.'

'William Barnes.' He did not offer his hand.

Then Ted asked a question he had not prepared, or so much as sensed was within him to be asked. He heard it spoken as if by another, and was startled.

'Would you have any work?'

Plates clattered briefly inside the kitchen but the farmer was silent, looking at him steadily. Ted looked back.

'What sort of work might that be?'

'Farm work.'

'You've done that?'

'No.'

'No.'

After a minute, Ted turned away, feeling ashamed.

'Say your name again?'

'Ted Howker.'

'All right, Ted Howker, come here tomorrow. I can use a hand with the ewes. Don't know about permanent.'

* * *

He did not go back home for hours, but wandered about the hills and on, further than he had ever been in his life, fretting about whether to tell them at home. He found a stream which had a last dribble of brackish water in the bottom and wet his hands and face though he dared not risk drinking from it. The heat had congealed like oil. When he came near a sheep he looked at it carefully, though the animal always ambled a few yards further off, eyeing him. He did not know which were the ewes.

But he knew that whatever the work among them was like and whether he had any aptitude for it, everything about it would be better than being crammed against twenty other men in a cage and sent grinding down the shaft to the hot black tunnels. Until earlier that year he had never given it much thought, simply because the reality of it had seemed further away than his present span of years. His days and his attention were filled with the life of home and school and of the terraces and with the routine of days. And then time speeded up, he was fourteen and the pit was waiting for him.

He reached home to mayhem and his mother in hysterical tears.

'I never thought. I never thought.'

'Well, you should have flaming well thought,' John Howker said and fetched Ted such a crack across the side of his head that his ears sang. He had not had such a blow since he was nine years old and it was the humiliation that pained him most.

'Look at your mother, and you to blame. How did you not think?'

It was long enough since Arthur had walked out and never come back or sent a word for Ted to have truly forgotten, but to his mother, his disappearance for half a day was simply the same terrible loss over again and Arthur's as if it was last week.

He stumbled through telling them where he had been and what he had done but no one listened. His father brushed his words aside and sat down to his tea, his mother put the dishes on the table in between wiping her eyes over and over again, though they were quite dry now. It bewildered him that they could have missed him and been in such a fret over his absence, and now that he was here, appear not to care about him at all, as if his return were the outcome of some trick but his actual presence of no account.

He waited until his father stood up and folded his newspaper, ready for bed. Clive was in from the pit and snoring, Evie packing the next day's bait. And then he told them. At first they thought he had found work for the twelve days of holiday left before the pit and were pleased, even though the question of payment had not been mentioned by William Barnes, so that Ted could not tell them how much he would be bringing home. But then he plucked up enough courage to tell them again.

'I'll work there for good. Instead of the pit. I'm never going underground, but I don't see how it matters where I work. It's all the same.'

His father's face went black. In the corner, Reuben's head bent further over the Bible and his muttering from Job was like far distant thunder. John Howker tore at his son until Evie pulled them apart.

'What's the difference?' Ted kept crying out.

'Difference is this is a pit family and you are one of it, that's the difference.'

'And Arthur ran away before he'd go down there another time.'

This time the crack across his head almost felled him.

But he got up before light the next morning and left the house without anyone preventing him and that was the beginning of his time working on the hills beyond Mount of Zeal.

8

WHEN ROSE had been married for two years and there was still no pregnancy, people, as they always did, made remarks and hinted to Evie, and before much longer began to ask one another if all was well, not with Rose's health but with her marriage. Ida Minns commented in this way, first to her husband and daughter, then to several friends. She did not speak to Rose because, in truth, she did not care for her daughter-in-law and had disapproved of the marriage from the outset. But she held Rose's mother in reserve, to speak to if things went on in the same way. And Evie Howker, being proud, would have listened in silence and sent her away and not only because she would not be patronised by the wife of a pithead manager. She had borne her own children without trouble – trouble came later, with too little money and too much grinding work as the backbone to four men. If Rose escaped any of it, even though she would also miss the short-lived joy of each baby, Evie could only envy her. Why Rose had not conceived she did not know and would not ask. Meanwhile, unhappy on her own all day in the empty house, Rose looked for work and found it behind the counter of the shop beside the Institute, from which the previous girl had been sacked and disgraced for thieving.

From the first morning she loved everything about the shop, loved the smells, the way the shelves were crammed with dozens of different items and yet always orderly, loved weighing out and filling up, loved the swish of the sugar into the cone of blue paper and the soft billows of flour, loved the meal sacks and the rattle of the coarse feed into the metal scoop, loved the cotton threads arranged in their colours on a rack and the smell of the balls of string and the shine on the boiled sweets. She felt as if the place behind the counter had been waiting for her to fill it. She had found more than work. People remarked that she looked well, her eyes were bright, her colour up, that she had 'something about her' and after a short time they forgot that Rose continued to be childless and, like Evie, they envied her.

Charlie Minns had moods when a livid humour weighed him down and to be rid of it he flailed about him, and in flailing, caught Rose on the side of her face. At the end of her first week in the shop he was early home because he had trapped his hand in a pulley, and although not broken, it was deeply bruised, and painful.

'I don't care for this,' he said. He was sitting at the table looking straight at Rose as she walked in. 'I like to come in to my food not an empty space and I would have done if you hadn't started as a shopworker.'

'I came out dead on half past five. Oh, Charlie, what have you done to your hand?'

He pulled it close to him as if he was afraid she would touch it. Rose felt guilt flood through her.

'I'm sorry, I'd have come home straight away. I'll set the kettle on first. Have you to be off sick?'

'I'm put in the office only, till it's healed.'

'Oh, that's good, that's a relief then.'

'Why? It isn't your hand.'

'No. I'm sorry.'

Rose had never said that she was sorry as many times in the whole of her past life as she had once she was married to Charlie. She could not get everything right, and some days got nothing at all. He had been spoilt, he had moods, rages and then bouts of hunched-up silence, when he would not look at her or speak. At other times he would be funny, affectionate and kind. She never knew which Charlie to expect.

She had no child simply because none came and neither of them was troubled about it, Charlie because he knew a child would shift him from the centre of her attention, Rose because she had seen her mother worn out with all of them, together with John and Reuben, so the absence of one was not hurtful but the nods and behind-hand remarks were. She had trained herself to hold her head up and close her ears to them.

Now, as Charlie's moods became more melancholy and dispirited, and his behaviour towards her often angry and occasionally violent, she did not know whether to be happy that there was no child to suffer with her or sad because she faced him alone. No one knew what he was like, she spoke to no one and showed nothing on her face or in her responses. But the few days she had spent in the shop had given her a freedom which she knew that she would dread to lose. It did not strike her, in the way it might have done others, as a pathetically small or mean thing, this pleasure in working behind the counter, liking to guess whose face would come round the door as it opened and the bell rang, what they might buy today and what have to leave behind when the total added up to more than the contents of their purse. She only knew she felt happier than she had since early childhood, or on the few occasions when she and Mary had escaped to gossip and share secrets and a cigarette in the back field.

And now Charlie told her she had to give up the shop.

'I want you here when I come in.'

'Maybe I could try to change my hours, come home sooner. Yes, I'll ask for that.'

'I don't like my wife being a shop woman. Give in your notice tomorrow, Rose.'

She stood over him as he sat, mutinous and angry. He was small, his teeth were broken and rotting. His hair clumped greasily to his scalp. Rose shuddered with a realisation that she was bound to him for life, unless she was prepared to go slinking home in disgrace. She caught hold of a scrap of courage and clung to it as to a life belt. She said, 'I won't do that, Charlie. I don't see the reason why I should.'

'Reason is, I'm your husband and I'm telling you.'

But Rose's eyes were wide open now and she saw him for the small, ugly, bullying creature he was. She knew why she had married him. He was a manager's son and she had been flattered, and thought it the way to take a step up, as Mary had thought before her. She had wanted the married status they all naturally wanted, for what else was there? She had felt singled out and even important, though she had known so many were scoffing at her choice of man. She had been neither happy nor sorry and she had been spurred on by the thought of her own house and family. When the family did not come, she had still ducked away from facing her real future. Now, it was clear in front of her and she flinched from it.

She prepared their food and they ate it in silence, but now and then Charlie glanced at her sideways, his head low to his plate. It would be Christmas in five weeks and of course they were to go to his family, though Rose longed to be in Lower Terrace again, no matter if the room would be crammed full and Reuben would mumble his way through the Manger and the Shepherds and the Flight into Egypt over and over again. The Christmas and Easter stories were the only ones with the power to draw him away from the smiting and vengeance of the Old Testament.

Rose set down her knife and fork. 'I want to go home for Christmas,' she said.

'This is your home.'

'You know what I'm saying.'

But he did not reply, only scraped his plate round with the last lump of bread.

Rose cleared the table and took the pots out without saying any more.

9

ON A Sunday night in the hardest winter for twenty years, Ted came out of a mesh of blinding whiteness over dark and could feel neither his hands nor feet and with his face numb. When he tried to breathe, the air in his lungs crackled.

Slowly, he linked one thought to the next, one sensation to another, until he had a chain that made a pattern and knew where he was – in the farthest, topmost field, at the highest point, against a stony outcrop. It was dark, but the snow was vivid. There was a moon. The frost was like acid and he had his arms round a sheep, whose fleece was knotted into ropelets by the ice. His ears were ringing, the inside of his mouth tasted metallic. He lay still for several minutes with his eyes closed but when he felt himself falling down into icy sleep again he forced himself to look and saw the stars glittering above his head and a ring round the moon. No one was near. The sheep were clumped together in corners, half buried in snowdrifts. He had come out with William Barnes several hours ago, carrying hay, and plunged at once up to their waists in snow. After that, they had struggled against it to try and reach the flock who were farthest away and most deeply buried. The moisture on the bales froze as they moved.

Ted looked round but there was no sign of the farmer nor any other human shape in the shining expanse of snow. He managed to free his hands from the frozen sheep fleece and the animal fell forward into the drift, a dead weight. How many others were dead he had no way of knowing – those clinging to the scribble of hawthorn hedge on the far side might be frozen solid.

He must not let himself close his eyes again, or slip down into the warm hollow his body had formed in the snowdrift. If he did, he would freeze too.

The voices rang across the clear cold air, and then the figures came on, making a slowly moving pencil line across the snow, William Barnes, Joel Barnes, Aseph and Tom, neighbours from over the hill. They reached Ted and shouldered him, wrapping him in horse blankets and sacking, and struggled back through the dells they themselves had made on their way. Ted felt like a child being carried to bed, swaying as the men moved, the air dusting his face with powdery snow thrown up by their movement. By the time they got him into the farm kitchen and beside the fire, he was barely aware of his own body.

The next morning, he was left to sleep, and at ten o'clock in the snow-bright day, Gerda Barnes came up with a tray of tea and bacon. Ted lay in the white glare coming through the small window of the attic, and his limbs felt heavy and sore, his head oddly light. But he was alive and he would be up later.

'You stop in the house today, there's pots you can wash and potatoes to peel up and after that you'll be fit for nothing save more sleeping. Sheep,' she said with scorn on her way out, 'dang things are more trouble than they're worth and they're not worth a man's life.'

The winter petered out with little more snow and by February they were lambing. Ted was happy, loving the place, the wildness, the sheep, the work, content to be on his own or with William and Joel. He grew a couple of inches and his shoulders were broader. He changed from being a small, pale child to a young man strong as wire, and every day he woke wanting to be out on the hill, or to the barn with the ewes that had to lamb inside. The weather was kind after that last bout of bitter cold and snow, and the spring grass came fresh and early. He had no time to walk to Mount of Zeal, and no message came up for him, but when the main batch of lambs had arrived, he took a late afternoon off and went home. He heard the blower for the end of the shift as he walked along Paradise. A woman looked out of her door for the men coming up the slope, stared at him and ducked back inside. By the time he reached Lower the file was making its way up the track from the pithead. He saw his father and Clive, then Leonard the neighbour, walking together, and lifted his arm to them. They did not break stride. Ted stopped, troubled that his leaving could chill them towards him. He felt the fold of notes in his pocket.

Evie dished up the moment the men had their boots off and set behind the door. She was not surprised that they said nothing because food and tea came first, second and third, but when the pots were cleared, fresh tea made and John had settled in his chair, still not a word had been said. From the corner, Reuben's faint hoarse whisper read the story of the Tower of Babel. She looked from one man to the other, and not one of them met her eye and then she knew it was something to do with Ted, whose name John had ruled should never be mentioned in the house again. The bitterness hurt her so much that sometimes when she thought of it she could not catch her breath. She did not have words for how she missed her youngest child, the quiet, gentle boy who had spent so many of his days at the window looking out, but the space he had left was a hollow which she tiptoed round and kept warm for him.

And then, without the sound of a footstep or a hesitant tap on the door, Ted was in the room, shocking them into silent effigies of themselves, and even stopping the words that breathed from the black Bible and Reuben's mouth.

Something about his still presence and strength prevented his father from saying any of the things he had planned to say if ever he saw his son again, and had Clive look up at him and then away uneasily, in something like awe. He was Ted, the youngest, but another Ted, and they were hesitant before him.

Evie broke the atmosphere into shards by lifting the teapot and, because she trembled, chinking it against the cup until Clive reached out to hold it still, and after a minute, Reuben's voice squeaked into life again like a reedy instrument tuning up.

'Sit down,' John Howker said.

The fire drew badly, and Ted remade it. The kettle handle was bent and he took it off, straightened it, hammered it back. Clive went out, sullen of step.

Reuben slept, the black Bible slipping from his lap to the floor as it did every night.

'You're a stranger to us,' John said.

Ted pulled the fold of notes out of his pocket and set it on the table. No one moved to pick it up.

'It's about more than money.'

'All the same . . .'

'All the same,' Evie said, and swept the notes deftly into her hand and from there to her apron pocket. 'You've found a way of life you care for more than this one, that's clear. But don't look down at the ones who have to live beneath you because that's in the lie of the land only.'

'I know that. You'd be welcome to come.'

They looked at one another and looked away, and he knew that they would not.

Later, Evie set a fresh fruit cake on the table, with the usual slab of cheese, but after they had eaten, Ted got up, knowing that the early shift came round before you'd shut your eyes. He put out his hand to his father, who hesitated before he shook it, and touched Reuben's bald skull gently. Reuben did not stir. On the doorstep, he put his arm round Evie's shoulders but she only let it lie there for a second before turning.

In the house, putting the fruit cake back in the tin so old that its picture of Windsor Castle had rubbed almost away and only she knew what had been there with its tower and its flag, she thought but said nothing, only started to get Reuben ready for the night. But lying beside John Howker in the cold bedroom, under three blankets and the feather quilts, she said, 'He came back though. We know where he went and he came back and he'll come back again. Which Arthur has never done.'

John said nothing but the image of Arthur was between them in the darkness and they sensed all over again the hopelessness of it.

10

Sometimes when she was alone in the house Rose would switch on the wireless and find dance music, and be happy tapping and twirling about as best she could, in the spaces between the furniture. The chairs and sideboard and table had come from Charlie's grandmother's house and were old and ungainly, dark and ill-fitting in the small rooms.

She was dancing in this way, to a swing band, with the door open onto the street to let in some of the fresh spring air, when someone said, 'You shouldn't be dancing alone.'

He had his feet definitely on the path but his large body leaned inwards, so that Rose could hardly tell whether he was in the house or out of it and certainly he blocked out half the light.

She took a few steps back so that the table was between her and the leaning man.

'No, no, I didn't mean to upset you. I was going by. Heard the music.'

'Oh.' But she did not move from the protection of the table.

'I've moved to lodgings at the top.'

'Oh.'

'They call it Paradise.' He had large even teeth in his broad face, eyes like the coals.

'Where did you come from?'

'Stannett Valley. I like this better. You can see out.'

They both looked up towards Paradise and then the sky, though it was capped with thick oaten cloud now.

He laughed.

'You're at the pit,' Rose said.

He nodded, tipped his cap back, showing a doormat of hair.

She wanted to ask his name but dared not, and then his bulk shifted and the light came back into the room.

She thought nothing of it until later, when Charlie had taken himself to bed with a pouring cold, and she was setting the pots out for the morning, and then the man's frame in the doorway and the way he had stood there and spoken as if he had known her all her life came to her and she stopped as she took a cup from the rack, and held it in mid-air. Nothing unplanned or unexpected happened in Mount of Zeal, unless it was a sudden death. New faces were few, passers-by unknown.

She had decided to defy Charlie and stay at the shop, so in the end that door too opened on the man she had learned was called Lem Roker. He joined the shuffling queue of those coming off the late shift, buying tobacco and a newspaper, shaving soap and matches, and when he stood in front of her she did not know whether to look at him or away.

'You could dance in here,' he said, 'when it's quiet.'

Rose looked away.

That Friday, Charlie's mother was taken ill suddenly and into hospital twenty miles away. Charlie went with his father, telling Rose in one breath that it was nothing, in the next that she might die that same night, terrified and panicking. She put up a small bag for him, was worried and at the same time full of scorn that he was still his mother's boy, and his distress was about himself, about her leaving him, and did not arise out of deep concern for her.

He left the house without a word and Rose had to run after him with the bag, which he grabbed as if his leaving it were her fault. She went back, cleared up and sat for a while, her hands together, knowing that she did not care, because her mother-in-law had never made a secret of her scorn, never welcomed or accepted her, never failed to criticise something she said or did or wore or cooked, every time they met. Why should she be troubled about her illness, which would surely turn out to be trivial?

And then she heard footsteps going past the door, and after a moment, more footsteps, and voices, and as she heard them she jumped up, knowing that she was going where they were going, and would not listen to any whispers from her conscience. She got ready quickly, knowing that excitement and daring made her flush prettily, knowing that she had the courage to defy them all.

The hall was crowded by the time she walked in, the chatter and the music from the band and the tap of heels on the wooden floor jerking it to life. But when Rose was seen the gradual quiet that came over them, and the stillness, so that only the music went on, was shocking. People turned, looked, turned away and to one another. She edged round the room and their eyes followed her. She tried to catch this or that person's attention but though they were all looking none of them saw her. She went to the hatch from which the drinks were served and asked for a lemonade.

Roy Parris, who was serving, pulled off the cap, slid it over the counter and waited for the money, all in complete silence, but as Rose fidgeted in her purse, a hand came down on the wooden ledge with the correct coins, picked up the bottle and gave it to her. Then he took her elbow, led her to a seat in the far corner, and after that, still standing, looked round the entire hall, at every face, slowly.

There was a jerk into life again, people took hold of one another and went onto the floor to dance, the band quickened up. They had lost interest in her, or pretended to.

'You like dancing,' Lem Roker said, 'so finish that and we'll dance.'

'I shouldn't dance, not tonight.'

'Why else did you come?'

Why else?

She sensed that someone was looking at her. Mary, a few yards away, eyes on Rose's face, telling her not to dance, not to stay in a corner alone with Lem Roker, urging her to leave. Rose looked away.

Mary watched them dance, following every move, and without glancing at her Rose knew what her expression said. Mary was right but now the band was playing with even more life and energy and she loved this dancing. Lem, was good at it for all his size, quick on his feet and with an easy rhythm. People watched them and forgot to look away and Rose felt defiant and light as air.

He would walk her home, he said, and what did it matter if they were noticed and remarked upon, she might not be safe alone.

Rose laughed. 'It's safe enough here. Nothing ever happens.'

'Nothing at all.' Then they both laughed and he would have taken her arm, but they had neared the corner from which they could see her house, and the light on in the front window.

'Charlie.' She pulled away from Lem and flew down the street, hearing voices of others coming from the Institute but not daring to glance back.

11

THEY WERE sitting in the midday sun, can of tea between them, cheese and bread and pie just crumbs on the slab of rock.

'That was a good day when you found your way up here,' William said. Ted drained his tea and wiped his mouth. The July warmth fed his bones. He had no need to reply. They both knew. Whenever he clambered down the steep track home he felt the walls closing in on him and his spirit shrivel and darken. He went for his mother's sake. If she had not been there he would never have left the farm.

He lay on his back, arms behind his head. William was trying to get his pipe to light. The sheep were quiet. Afterwards, Ted's single frozen moment of memory was of the quietness, the heat of the sun, the smell of the first thin plume of tobacco smoke, the taste of tea in his mouth, the firmness of the ground beneath him. They seemed to be caught and held. Time had stopped. But that was afterwards.

The sound of the explosion rocked the hill, as if it had happened in the earth immediately below them but then broken open the sky too. The reverberations went on and on. The sheep took off, bleating wildly, surging away up the steep track. William was on his feet first, Ted scrambling up while he was still bewildered by the vastness of the sound. William was yards ahead of him while Ted was standing like a boulder.

'Run, boy, run.'

'What happened?'

'Pit explosion,' the farmer shouted over his shoulder, slipping and almost falling on the dry track, recovering his balance and bounding on. 'Run, boy!'

Ted ran.

Every door stood open, every man and woman in Mount of Zeal who had use of their legs was making for the pithead, men who five minutes before had been asleep pulled on clothes as they ran, women scooped babies out of cribs and carried them swaddled, and dragged small children. William and Ted were behind but they caught up and raced on down, Ted jumping over walls and taking steps three at a time. The whole area round the machinery was filling up. Men were surging forwards, shouting out that they had come to help, where should they go, women edged close to one another and simply stood. There were shouts, and then vehicles and gear and fire engines, then the whole paraphernalia of disaster attendance. Police came, held people back, shouted at the women not to go nearer.

No one knew, no one came forward to explain, no one had time. Murmurs went round, rumour after rumour flew.

Ted and William Barnes were pushed back.

'Nothing you can do yet, they're sending the search crews down, nothing you can do.'

Ted looked round for his father and mother, saw neither at first but then there was his mother, scarf to her face, eyes huge with fear. He reached her and she clung to him, hardly breathing, her body like a rod.

And after that, all they could do was stand and wait, as the cages went down and eventually came up again, teams emerged, returned, went to report. They stood hour after hour and for the most part they were all silent. Only a child called here and there, or a baby wailed. Once, a dog set up howling like a terrible banshee and would not stop until someone threw a brick and it fled, tail down. A few went away and came back with tins of tea. Children were taken home.

School had been let out as soon as the blast came. But the inner core of women whose men were below stayed, silent, grey-faced, watching, watching. Waiting.

It fell dark and they brought storm lights and the lights turned the women's faces moon-coloured and hollowed out their eyes.

It had been clear but after midnight cloud trailed across the sky, thickened and ballooned out. A thin rain fell.

More cans of tea came, and rough-cut slabs of bread and cheese, chunks of fruit cake. More tea. The rescuers stood briefly, downing pint after pint of it and scoffing handfuls of food before getting into the cages and descending again to the hell below.

It went on until dawn. But as a wan light stained the terraces of Mount of Zeal, the lift came up once more and unloaded men whose skin was stained worse than coal black, and who smelled of acrid smoke. And then the lift gates stayed open. No one else went down. A couple of wagons started, revved and drove away. A gang of firemen stood hopelessly together, helmets on the ground beside their feet.

A woman started to keen aloud, and another took up the crying, but they were both shushed into silence, for the noise unnerved the rest of them.

Ted encouraged his mother to turn for home, but she was riveted to the spot where she had first settled and would not shift. He looked round to try and see William Barnes, even while knowing that the farmer must have gone back up the hill hours before. He should go back too. But Evie's hand was fierce on his arm and he could not leave her.

Word went round at noon and by then soup had been brought and bread and jam and cake. More tea, with a snuff of brandy for the women who had to wait for the final word. They knew too well but could not go until it was given out loud.

The minister came and read prayers and Ted listened to words from the Bible that were stitched into him. Someone sounded a note and the hymns began, slow and hesitant then rising and swelling until they filled the village and rose up and out to the hill beyond.

It began to rain harder, and then to pour. Scarves were tied more tightly on heads, coats drawn round. But they stayed. Evie had not released Ted's arm for hours, perhaps was not even aware of its being there, but he felt that pulling himself away would tear the skin from her, as if they had been born melded like this and become one.

Just before four o'clock, the pit owner stood on a platform hastily made from a trolley. Those who were left, perhaps thirty or forty people, stood as silent as when a coffin is lowered into the ground.

He was grey, and sweat poured down his face and neck. His voice was unsteady as he read from a sheet of paper handed to him.

The explosion had started an immediate fire, and there had been a sudden collapse and fall of rock at the same time, making two disasters in one. Rescue workers had brought nine miners to the surface. Two died before they reached the air, one as they put him into the ambulance. Four were taken to hospital. Their bodies were variously broken and burned, and even where their injuries were less severe, the shock could still kill them.

Ten men died underground, and because of the fire and the rock fall, rescue attempts had been abandoned. The lives of the fire crew and others were at too great a risk. Orders had been given for the tunnel and chamber to be sealed and left, an outcome everyone in a pit village dreaded and would have given their own lives to avoid. But sometimes, there was no other way and everyone knew that too. The men had lived, died and been buried and the mine must be their grave.

James Green
Isaac Howes
Richard Belby
Peter Mates

Joel Dunn
James Sawyet
Silas Fermor
John Howker
Clive Howker
Jimmy Howker

PART THREE

12

THERE WERE close on two hundred sheep and he went to them one by one, even those that were up on the top outcrop which took some scrambling to reach.

William Barnes watched him from the farm gate. He had known the day would come but had hoped against it, not only because Ted was a good worker and had fitted from the start, but because he loved the place and the animals as if they were his own and had never had a bad day. The time he was half frozen to death had been all he had taken off work and even then he had struggled out before he was properly right.

William sucked on his empty pipe, not being due any tobacco until two days hence. He could find another worker but his heart wasn't in it, not only because one as good would be hard to come by but because he would miss Ted's quiet, steady company. He could not speak about it, as he had not been able to say a word against the boy's leaving. He had a duty in Mount of Zeal now his father and brothers were killed and sealed into their death chamber. His mother needed the wage, his sister was living at home and unlikely to get other work because of the shame that had had her dismissed from behind the shop counter. There might be a bit of money in compensation for the accident, but everyone knew how long that took, if it ever came in at all.

He saw Ted coming down the track towards him, his face fallen in and brooding with the misery he felt. He reached the gate and stood beside William, and looked out at the hill, and neither of them could speak.

He was due to go the next morning but while they were still in bed they heard a faint click of the back door latch.

Gerda touched her husband's side. 'He couldn't bear to leave by the light,' William said.

And it was in darkness that Ted reached the house on Lower, and slipped into his old room and lay on his unmade bed, and stared at the ceiling until morning.

He was taken on at the pit and started the day they opened up again after the explosion and he dreaded going down into the bowels of the mine, and feared what he might see, and the fact that he would be shut in and close to the charred bodies of his father and brother. But he was sent a distance away, along quite a different working, and in any case, the end that had been blown up had been sealed completely and was not identified, save on papers in the management office. Ted would never know.

They set him to work with the ponies at first so that he felt comfortable at once, though he pined, as he believed they did, for the light and air. He hated the taste in his mouth and the thick black dust he breathed in, and the smell on his skin.

Evie had found him when she had come down to the kitchen early on his first morning back, and silently put her arms round him.

'Will you stay tonight, Ted?'

'I'm staying for good.'

She had looked at him sharply. 'No. I've lost too many.'

'You have me back.'

'And how long before that pit swallows you?'

'First accident for forty years and you know it.'

'And not the last. That pit is cursed now.'

'That's superstition. You need the wages, you need me here.'

He had set the kettle on and now it shrieked at them, breaking into their angry talk. Evie went to it, not wanting there to be anger but, all the same, unable to stop it from overwhelming her, when she thought about the mine, even more powerfully than her grief.

Reuben's voice had been silenced now. He sat, holding the black Bible on his lap, forming the words but only air came from his mouth. He was shrunken small and bent and thin as a twig so that the chair engulfed him. But when Ted came into the room his eyes brightened and he fumbled through the thin paper of the Bible pages to find verses the boy had always liked to hear. When he had them he nodded his head until Ted came over, sat down and took the book from him.

'*When I consider thy heavens, the work of thy fingers, the moon and the stars, which thou hast ordained . . .*'

Reuben rested his head against the chair back and closed his eyes.

Ted read until his grandfather was asleep, lulled by the words as he had been lulled by them as a child. He had never known what they meant and he did not think he knew now. It did not matter. The words were the background to his entire growing up and woven into his life like another skin. He realised that he had missed nothing of home during his time at the farm but he had noticed the spaces where the words had been.

13

ROSE HAD done nothing more than dance with Lem and let him walk her home, and once he had been waiting for her when she left the shop, and walked back with her then. She had made no secret of it and been defiant in her belief that she had done nothing wrong, and if anyone wanted to tell Charlie, let them. He barely needed telling. Word about something of this sort was breathed out onto the air and breathed in again by everyone else in turn until it reached the person for whom it was intended.

Charlie had thrown everything she had brought with her to his house onto the street, Rose herself last of all, and barred the door against her. That had been a week before the pit disaster and which had been worse for Evie Howker to bear could not be told.

Rose had come home in shame but John and Clive had gone down within five minutes to pick up her things and lug them home, to try and put a limit on her disgrace. If everyone knew what had happened at least they would not be given the satisfaction of having clothes and a trunk, a bedspread and an embroidered tablecloth to gaze upon and pick over. Once they had finished and shut the door again on family privacy, John Howker had told Rose that he could not have turned her away but that he could not welcome her either. 'I'll put up with you, but I can never like it. I'll give you a roof again but I can never think of you as anything but a lodger.'

She could not have borne to return to her married home, but she was a stranger in Lower Terrace, her father barely speaking to her, Evie shaking her head and drawing in her breath every time she looked at her. If Ted had been there it would have been easier. Only Reuben knew nothing of what had gone on and showed no interest in her return.

On the day of the explosion she was in the scullery when the men went, had packed their bait tins and set out their boots, as if she were twelve years old again and obliged to help Evie with every chore. The men had gone without a word, though Clive had glanced back and caught Rose's eye and forever afterwards she was sure that he had winked at her, though if he had it was for the very first as well as the last time.

When she had heard Ted's voice from below, she had stayed in her room. Evie must tell him. The deaths of the men, the way the disaster had seemed to explode not just part of the coal mine but the lives of everyone in Mount of Zeal, had made Rose's crisis fade almost to invisibility. She had been needed by Evie, she had taken over the house and looking after Reuben and her mother without a word, and when she went out, no one looked at her in the old way – perhaps they did not even see her. A household whose men have been taken in a pit disaster is not only marked out, it is spared any comment or criticism of any kind, and for good.

She went down now and found Ted washing the pots.

'Rosie.'

He was the only one ever to call her this and he did not do so often. Now, it overwhelmed her with sadness.

'I suppose you've heard it all.'

'Enough.' He turned to find the tea towel but she had it already.

'I've done nothing wrong, Ted. I know what's believed about me but I'm the only one to know the truth.'

'And him.'

'Lem.'

'You've a husband, Rose.'

'Don't come like that to me. I know well what I have and what kind of a man I married.'

Ted stopped her arm as it reached for another plate to dry. 'Did he beat you?'

'No, no. I'd have left long since. I would never let a man be rough to me, you should know. I'd have come home and . . .' Tears came without warning. 'Told Dad. Told Clive or Jimmy.'

'Told me.'

'You weren't here to tell, you were over the hill on a farm, weren't you?'

'It's not across the sea, Rosie. I would have come. I'd have had his head off if he'd touched you.' He crushed an eggcup in his hand. It snapped off its stem. 'What will you do?'

'Look after Mam, look after you.'

She saw Ted, the small brother grown a man and her grandfather an old one grown small again. Charlie's face and hands and hair were not coated with coal grime, looking after him had not been like looking after a man such as John Howker and the brothers had been. And now Ted. Lem was a pitman, looked after by a landlady, which could not be the same and did not seem right.

'I don't say you have to stay with a man who doesn't do right by you,' Ted said slowly, as if working it out before he spoke, 'but I don't say you should be seen with any other.'

'You know nothing about any of it.'

'No. I expect I don't. But I know you, Rose, and I want you to keep your good name. What will you and Charlie do? Divorcing is a terrible thing.'

'Why?'

Ted shook his head, not able to give words to the momentousness of it.

'So I'm to stay at home for ever?'

He did not answer.

'Charlie won't be long on his own. He wanted me out, he'll want someone new in, and there are plenty who would go. He's a manager. He stays above ground. He stays clean.'

Evie had gone to bed. She went to bed in the daytime often now, being unable to bear the living breathing world. She slept with the covers up over her face, hour after hour, and slept again through a long night. Reuben slept too, the black Bible slipping off his knees onto the floor with a thump that never disturbed him into waking, though sometimes he gave a little moan, or a sob.

'I wish you weren't down the pit,' Rose said quietly. 'I fear for you every day.'

Ted shook his head. 'We've had our turn.'

'Doesn't follow. Wouldn't you rather be up there, out in the open with the sheep?'

'Yes.'

'Then you should go back.'

He left the room without a word. But when Rose went out just after eight o'clock that Friday night, he stood at the window watching her go and nursing a dark tight fear inside himself, because she was meeting Lem Roker and he believed that she would flaunt herself with him carelessly at the Institute rooms. He had known little of Charlie and that little he had not greatly liked, but he wanted order in a world which had so recently been blown apart and scattered and his sister's marriage represented that order.

Just before half past eleven he went out. The night smelled cold and the trails and whorls of stars were mirror bright in the dark sky. The music of the band came up the terrace through the open windows and door. Ted leaned back into the shadows when it stopped and almost at once people started to come out, talking and laughing. There were plenty before Rose and Lem Roker and then they came out, sidling past a gang of others who were singing. The man's hand was on her arm. Ted waited. Watched. Followed. And then they were out of sight, somewhere away from the rest and shielded by the darkness.

He did not know what to believe. If Rose had told him the truth, then he had no worry and he should not be following them. If she had not, what could he do? But he felt it keenly that he was the only man in the Lower Terrace house now, the only one to defend his sister against the spiteful tongues and stand up for her to Evie. The only one Rose could rely on. But perhaps she neither needed nor wanted him.

The dancers separated and floated home like clouds parting and being blown away, and in minutes the lights had gone out in the Institute rooms and Mount of Zeal was silent again. The stars burned bright and cold.

14

IT WAS well into autumn before Ted was on Lem Roker's shift. It came about one September dawn when he was walking through the soft air and thinking of how it smelled and how it would be on the hill among the sheep, how their coats would be pearled with drops of moisture and the spiders' webs dewy on the gate. The mist would be a ghostly shawl over the high ground.

The sound of his boots joined that of all the others making their way down the terraces to the hollow where the pithead workings loomed up, and then he saw Lem not far ahead, his height and odd rolling walk marking him out from the rest. In the press of men going down in the cage Ted was on the far side from him, but at the crossroads the foreman pointed.

'With Roker and Leach on Nine Avenue. Your lamp's not set straight.'

They were flat out all morning and spoke little, though the usual jokes went to and fro, and the warnings were shouted above the racket of the carts going down. Ted was still not used to the heat and the dense closeness of the air. Sweat ran down his body from the time they got down to the time they arrived back at the top. Roker watched him, corrected this or that, but Ted had learned fast and needed little supervision now. They both had their heads down and barely made contact.

The trouble started up after they stopped to eat. Roker was a dozen yards away across the truck rails, sitting on the floor. Ted ate with his back against an outcrop, his bait tin on the ground beside him, his tea can already empty. Thirst was the first thing they had to slake. Food came way behind. Two men had a dice game going on the floor. Roker and several others were bandying words about women. Ted barely listened. The heat made him so tired he almost fell asleep as soon as he sat down every day. The rest were used to it.

It was his sister's name that woke him.

'I heard about that, Lem Roker. You're a sly one.'

'Why?'

'Still married to a manager is Rose.'

'I know that. Married but not married.'

Ted stood up but it was dark between them and they hadn't noticed him.

'You're not telling me she'd look at you.'

'Family's a pit family. Why not?'

But it was too close to talk of the disaster and deaths and no one allowed it below. Ted waited but they went on to some other thing, the management, the way you could be cheated, the likelihood of flooding, new safety rules. He hesitated, then returned to his place and packed up his bait tin. A minute later, the bell sounded.

He wanted to tackle Rose as soon as he got home but she had taken the bus with Evie to buy winter coats, the first for seven years, and by the time they got back Ted was asleep in bed. The next day and the next he was on early shift. It was Thursday before he was alone with his sister.

'It was only jesting,' Rose said. 'Men say anything to make themselves big.'

'I don't like to hear those things said about you. It brings disgrace. It makes people turn and stare.'

'Let them.'

'You don't mean that. You hate it when there's tattling tongues, you always said so. I hate it, Rosie. We've never had anything to be ashamed of.'

'Still haven't. I'm not going without any fun or attention. Maybe you should try that.'

'It was the way he talked about you.'

'Lem means no harm. Leave it alone. And don't say any word to Ma.'

He had fully intended to put it from his mind. Rose was a grown woman so he had better interfere no more. But the week after, Lem was talking again, this time as they were pouring out of the gates and up the slope to home. He was a few behind Ted but his voice carried and he was laughing about taking Rose to the dance that Friday.

'You're one for tripping to the music,' someone said. 'Never saw what that was about.'

'Not the music though, is it, Lem?'

Laughter. Ted broke step with his own companions and walked slowly to hear the others better.

'It is and it isn't.'

'Get on. I've seen you.'

'Nice and easy, Rosie. Married woman, isn't she.'

Ted reached him, and stood in his path. The others slowed and hesitated, looking uneasy.

'Who are you, Lem Roker? You take what you just said back or I'll ram it down your throat.'

There were murmurs. 'Steady on.' 'Now then, Ted.' 'Leave it alone, boy.' But he swung round on them with his fists up and they retreated, save for Robbie

Calder who took his arm and urged him away. Ted shook him off. Lem Roker stood his ground, smirking.

'Take back what I just heard you say about Rose.'

'Or?'

More muttering. 'Ted, leave it. Let it drop, he didn't mean anything.'

'He meant everything. Now take it back.'

Now Roker laughed. 'Young Ted. Trouble is, you're wet behind the ears, you know nothing but sheep and sheep don't teach you the facts of life.'

His laugh was taken up by others and one or two had come back to find out what was happening. But still the sensible few were urging Ted away.

'Take back what you said or I'll do for you, Lem Roker.'

Lem roared with laughter, throwing his head back, his open mouth showing fine strong teeth.

'I've nothing to fear from you, boy Ted, and besides, why should I take back the truth? Rose is a nice easy girl and ready for whoever wants her and you know it.'

The blow Ted struck had his full weight behind it but that weight could not have caused such damage – he had grown and he was stronger, but he was still slight, more nerve and sinew than muscle and strength. But he hit out straight and quickly, catching Lem off balance and causing him to stagger backwards and fall, and in falling, hit the side of his head on the low boundary wall. It made a cracking sound like stone on stone and the man lay still instantly, leaden, without a twitch or a breath. A trickle of blood wound like a worm from behind his ear and crawled over the path.

There were a few seconds of terrible silence and then Ted ran. It seemed that he ran as fast as man or boy had ever run, bounding up the paths from terrace to terrace until he reached Paradise and then he was away and out of sight, and the men were all turned to the body of Lem Roker, for body they knew that it was and no longer a living breathing man. One went to the pit foreman's office and the telephone, two others knelt and put a jacket under the head, another bent to listen for the faintest breath or heartbeat. The rest of them just stood about, grey-faced, and then front doors and windows were opened and women began to come out. And in all the time it took for the doctor to arrive, not one of them made a move to go after Ted, who had killed and run away.

PART FOUR

15

ROSE CAME every week to the prison, travelling by bus and train and taking hours.

'I never expected to see you again,' Ted told her the first time. And it was the truth.

'It was a dreadful mistake, that's all. You were standing up for me and there was an accident.'

Ted had felt his fist connect with Lem Roker's jaw, bone on bone, and then the sound of his head as it hit the stone. He would have done the same thing again so it was surely not an accident, but neither had he meant to kill the man. He regretted running away, too, the moment he stood by the farm gate, his chest heaving as he tried to get his breath. He had gone mad and now he had come to. There had been a couple of men coming up the track to fetch him and he had saved them the trouble of climbing further by waving his arms and going towards them. Neither of them had spoken and they had not attempted to restrain him in any way. They had simply walked together back into the village and every house door had been open and in every doorway someone stood watching, watching, in silence.

Evie had been with Rose inside the house, Evie weeping, Rose white-faced and holding herself stiffly as if she kept her limbs together only with the greatest effort.

'What have you done, what have you done, Ted?'

'I wasn't hearing him say those things. I couldn't let him talk like that, how could I?'

Rose had stood up then and put her arms tightly round him and the strength and warmth of her had said everything to him. He was to know it again only once more in his life.

'Grandfather's voice came back to him,' Rose said now. 'We hadn't told him anything but people came into the house and of course he heard everything, and one night he started to read aloud again.'

She was twisting her gloves together, knotting the fingers and untying them and twisting them the other way.

'But maybe he never lost it. He just wanted to be silent.'

'Maybe.'

'There aren't any miracles, Rosie.'

He saw fear in her eyes.

'But you didn't mean it, you can't have meant it, so there's nothing to trouble you, is there?'

'I caused a man to die. I'll be kept in prison for a good long time.'

'But that's the . . .' She stopped and they did not dare to look at one another.

'Do they feed you well enough?'

'It's hot, it's plenty. You can't hope for home cooking.'

'No.'

'Never mind about me, what's happening to you? Are you back working in the shop?'

'They'd hardly have me now, would they?'

'Because you've a brother in prison? That's wrong, that's not your fault.'

'They see it as my fault. If I hadn't gone dancing . . .'

'So you stay at home with Mam all day.'

'I see Mary sometimes. She's been a good friend to me. I have to be at home for them, Ted. She's in no fit state. She cries a lot. She doesn't sleep at night.'

'I'm sorry. I wish I could tell her. Will you ask her to come, Rosie?'

But Rose shook her head. 'She couldn't do it. You haven't seen her these four months, you wouldn't know.'

'At least tell her I'm sorry. Do that.'

'I've said it to her. She doesn't take much in.'

'What do you mean? That her mind has gone?'

'Not that. She doesn't want to take it in. She doesn't want to talk about any of it.'

He knew what she meant now. He thought about it in the grey exercise yard, walking round the asphalt, and when he sat in front of his tin tray of dirty-looking potato and meat with thin gravy. He thought about it lying on his bunk hearing the clattering and clanging of footsteps on iron staircases and great metal doors and buckets and tins. She didn't want to hear his name. It was easier. She could shut out what had happened by shutting out him until in the end she forgot he had ever been. If she so much as asked a question about him when Rose returned from visiting it would bring him back to life and she wanted him dead to her.

She would not attend his trial. Would Rose?

16

ROSE DID. She came every day of his trial, which was short, sitting in a place on the public benches where he could see her clearly. He got strength from that, as she had known he would. When he was brought into the dock, the first thing he did was look round until he saw her and waited for her to smile. He could tell how hard it was for her, how she had to force the smile and try not to look afraid.

They brought witnesses one after the other to speak against him, though they had in fairness to agree when asked that he had never been violent or angry previously, never to their knowledge started any fight or lashed out at a man. When Charlie Minns was called he gave Rose a mean and bitter look before telling lies about his wife and how she had behaved, how she had started going with Lem Roker almost as soon as setting eyes on him, neglected her home and duties, ignored her husband, been seen by countless people at different times on the man's arm, dancing with him, walking out. Ted saw his sister's face flush not with shame but with anger, and his own blood surged up to boiling inside him, so that once, the officer at his side sensed it and leaned over to warn him. Ted wanted to leap over and attack Charlie as he had attacked Roker, but when his turn came to go into the box, his words were clear and spoken out so that no one could fail to hear him. He had defended his sister, he said, and he was not sorry for that, and yes, he would defend her and her name and reputation as often as he had to against the slander and lies told. And yes, he had been angry, and wanted to teach Roker a lesson he would not forget, and yes, he had hit him. But no, he had never meant to kill him. He did not believe that he was capable of wanting to cause the death of any man.

From time to time Ted shuddered, with cold and with a flash of realisation – where he was, how he had come to be here, what was happening. What would happen. His counsel had been calm and serious but occasionally had grinned with uneven, yellowish teeth, through which he had said how sure he was that all would be well. Ted had reached out to clutch at his words and hold them tightly to him. The next time they met, the man had looked grave and not shown his teeth.

On the final day he began to have moments of being elsewhere, on the top of the hill in a high wind, in the shed bending over a distressed ewe, and then back in time, to his classroom and to the window seat in which he had sat day after day hearing Reuben reading from the black Bible. He was overwhelmed by the smells of each place, and the texture of things, the coarseness of the matted sheep's wool beneath his hand and the smokiness that filled the small front room when the coal fire did not catch right. He came to as if out of a deeply dreaming sleep each time, wondering where he was. But only for the blink of an eye. Reality was overpowering.

He listened carefully but the words made no sense. They were making speeches about him but they had nothing to do with him. The man they talked about was not even a man he knew.

And then there was a silence, and in that silence, he looked across at Rose. Her face was different, the eyes larger but sunken so far in that they were difficult to see. Her skin was the grey-white of the sheep's wool.

The jury had come back. The foreman answered the questions put to him.

More silence. Deeper silence.

And then a terrible mass intake of breath as the judge, sitting ahead and slightly above him, lifted the square of black silk. Ted, watching, saw that time slowed and every movement slowed so that it took hours for the black cap to be taken up and raised in the man's hand until it reached head level and then above the head and was put down to rest on the top of the wig, the wig which was the same colour as the fleece of the sheep, too, and there it rested, hideously dark, hideously still, indelible.

Hours passed before the judge spoke, and in those hours, Ted was in a vortex of the past, in school, in the scullery, in his grandparents' house on Paradise, beside Alice who was dying and then dead, on the terraces winding down Mount of Zeal, in the cage inching down to the Devil's pit, on the hill, in the drift of heavy snow and frozen to the gate, and in the bedroom at the farm with the snow blinding white on the white wall. His ears rang.

'. . . you are sentenced to be taken hence to the prison in which you were last confined and from there to a place of execution where you will be hanged by the neck until dead . . .'

17

Mount of Zeal drew in upon itself, Lower melding with Middle, and Paradise seeming to bend down and embrace them. There were no divisions now and not a paper to put between households in their concern for the Howkers. Evie was watched over and tended to night and day by this woman or that, cleaning done, food prepared and cooked or brought hot on trays under white cloths. Rose worked with whoever came, from morning till night, and in the night, sat at the window looking out, as Ted had always done, her conscience shredded by what was her fault in the end and only hers. She ate little, went from cushion to wishbone in a few weeks, as if the flesh had been scraped away. Evie scarcely spoke but sat all day with her head bent, or stood at the open doorway, staring, staring above Paradise to the green-grey line of the hill. The doctor had given her a draught to help her sleep and it plunged her from full wakefulness into oblivion, and brought her back, like a diver to the surface, with the same ruthlessness.

There was nothing to be said and no one tried. The men went down in the cage every shift and returned with blackened faces and tramped up the terraces to home in silence and even the children were subdued on their straggling way to school, never rattling sticks along the railings, nor jumping with a wild shout off walls. Mount of Zeal waited in the shadow of death.

He was transferred to a prison further away, and on the journey he felt the road unwinding beneath the wheels of the van and this was another 'last time'. The engine running noisily, waiting for the gates to open. The engine being switched off and the way the van shuddered and went still.

The corridors. One two one two one two, dark blue back of the warder in front, moving fast, one two one two. He lost all sense of where he had been and where he was and where he would be going. Turn this corner, turn that, one two one two.

Stop.

It was different from anywhere he had been in the first prison, where he had a narrow bunk, a narrow cell in which the air itself seemed gravel-grey. This was larger, had a table, two chairs, a low bed. But the blanket was the same gravel-grey and the cupboard against the wall was brown wood, dark, varnished. The high window let in more light, though it was inner light from a courtyard between high buildings, not the true light of day.

He sat down at the table, the energy gone out of him like fast-flowing water down a sluice. The warder came and sat opposite, opened a drawer in the table and took out a pack of playing cards. Ted looked at them, strange objects from some other universe as they seemed to be.

'Game?'

He was heavy-shouldered, large-nosed, thick-fingered. At first he seemed to speak another language but slowly the meaning came up like lettering on a screen, and Ted understood.

He shook his head.

'You'll need to do something,' the man said. He spoke kindly. 'Read. Play a game with me or one of the others. You can ask for a jigsaw. You'll need to take your mind off things.'

But his mind was frozen and could never be freed again.

He had been in his old prison cell alone, with all the time in the world to think, but now he was not left, they changed duties, four of them, and he was never by himself in this world again.

He ate the food they brought, wrote a letter to Evie, one to Rose, one to William. The chaplain came in. The governor. He answered what questions they put to him and asked for nothing.

'You're entitled to a visitor, anyone of your family.'

His heart jumped, thinking of Rose. Rose would come and he longed to see her, almost as much as he longed for the hands of the clock to move backwards.

But he said, 'No. Thanks. No one.'

For he would not put her through that. It would be the cruellest thing he could ever do.

Reuben had taken to his bed for good some weeks earlier, and though the black Bible lay on the covers or the chair beside him, he no longer read it. Rose asked if he wanted her to find a passage for him but he shook his head with vehemence. No woman had ever read his Bible aloud to him. No woman ever would.

He started to talk a little, chatting in a soft and amiable voice to Alice, and called Evie or Rose Alice when he caught sight of them. He told Alice she was a good girl, that he had enjoyed his supper, that she baked a good loaf, that he was glad to sit beside her, and though there was never any word of love, hearing him, Rose knew that his words were full of it. Men in Mount of Zeal had never talked in a feeling way.

She ate little. She slept little. She thought only about Ted and had to force her mind round in the opposite direction for fear of letting the terrible imaginings flow in. But what was there left to think about? The past and the dead.

Reuben died one night. Rose found him, cold as stone, when she came down at seven. He had never asked after Ted, as he had never asked after any of the others, seeming to accept each disappearance without the need for comment. She folded his hands and set the black Bible between them.

He had made little noise for months but the house with just Evie and herself was now silent, an emptiness where he had so long been.

Just women in the end, Rose thought. Evie was on the settle, knitting her fingers together. She did not know how much her mother thought about what was happening, whether she had let her mind go blank, and of course no one who came in to them spoke of it. Looks were all they gave.

18

THAT NIGHT, William Barnes went out onto the hill among the sheep at ten and stayed there, knowing he would not sleep in his bed. He moved among the animals, touching one here and there, went to the top of the slope and sat, walked across to the far side, and sat again. One or two of the sheep ambled nearer so that he could feel the warmth of their breath on the air around him.

He could not think of what was to happen, nor not think of it. He thought of Ted, the day he had arrived up here, of Ted when they had carried him back half-frozen stiff, of Ted rubbing a newborn lamb with a handful of straw to make it cough the mucus from its lungs to breathe.

He had heard the story a dozen times. What had happened had happened, that was plain enough, but that Ted had meant it to happen, had hit out meaning to kill, he could never accept. Anger might have killed, anger or accident. Not intent.

But it had come to this in the end and nothing had made a difference.

He could not make sense of it and for the first time in his adult life, in the darkness, he wept and then sat, simply waiting for the morning.

They had given him food but he had not eaten, and whisky which he had asked for but not drunk. The warder had tried to tempt him with the playing cards again but Ted's hand had been shaking so much he had knocked the pack onto the floor and they had pattered down everywhere, sliding under the table and chairs and slipping into a corner and touching the front of the wooden cupboard. They had got down on their hands and knees to retrieve them but the warder had grabbed most and made Ted get back onto the chair.

His bed was made but he did not lie on it.

The chaplain had been and spoken to him and then read out of the Bible, a passage about mercy which Ted knew by heart, having heard Reuben say it aloud a hundred times or more. His lips had mouthed the words with the priest, who had looked at him intently, before reading on. He had asked if there was anything he had to say, or ask, or tell, and Ted had opened his mouth to cry out in terror and anguish and pleading, but he could make no sound come.

The governor had been and tried his best to give him courage and Ted had felt for him because of the horror his job forced him to endure but the courage did not come. All night, his bowels kept opening until he thought there could surely be no waste left in his body. But still it came.

The doctor came, with brandy, which he was suddenly greedy for and drank down so fast it took his breath and made him choke. He held out the glass and, after hesitating, the man poured more. Ted set it on the table in front of him. When they came for him he would swallow it, at the last minute, before he was taken again down the endless narrow corridors.

There were no corridors. He was almost asleep, and in the claws of a nightmare, sitting at the table with his head in his hands, when he was wakened by the warder's hand on his arm, shaking him hard, and then by the opening of the door. Two men entered, a tall warder behind a man of middle height, slight, with a small moustache. He wore a dark suit with a smart white handkerchief in the top pocket.

Ted did not know where he was or what was happening, until his own warder handed him the brandy he had kept. 'Drink it up quick,' he said softly. He held it for him while he drank, as if Ted were a baby, because his hand shook too much. This time, though it burned his gullet, it did not choke him.

'Follow me please.'

The wooden cupboard had been pushed sideways. It slid easily, as if oiled. Ted hesitated, then stepped behind the man into the room beyond.

And it was here. No corridors. No keys. Here. The small room.

Time did not stop or go backwards, time went on in the old steady way, but so little time, seconds, before he was standing where the man told him, the chaplain was making the sign of the cross, there was another man binding his arms, then bending down, and before another second had gone there was a strap tying his legs together. His bowels heaved and opened. He screamed but the scream was muffled by the cloth bag over his head, over his face.

A muffled click and his head cracked open, as if it were hitting stone and the light inside the bag went out.

www.vintage-books.co.uk